Funeral at Lone Bull

Monty Bassett

*

I couldn't read until I was sixteen! And though raised in a family of cowboys and cowgirls, where storytelling was the preferred entertainment in the evening, if it wasn't for my Mother's insistence that I learn to read and wife Nicole, the stories and my courage to tell them would have died with the dwindling flames of a campfire.

*

SETTING:

The Town of Lone Bull sat, or rather hung, on a bench halfway up the steep slopes of Lone Bull Mountain. The name originally came from a gold miner named Elijah Cornfield who found a nugget of gold in a high alpine stream running down the mountain and out into Kolsana Lake. The name was derived from a single bull caribou who co-inhabited the mountain with Cornfield until winter, when the miner shot him for food.

Cornfield did well digging into the mountain, following the nugget's parent seam, but once, having made his fortune he moved to San Francisco after selling his claim to a large mining company. The company was a big industrial operation with giant motorized jackhammers on machines so large, that the cutting teeth on the buckets were ten meters from the operator.

So confident was the mining company that the vein was massive that a town named Lone Bull was formed,

To accommodate the few dozen residences of the town; a general store, a hardware store, a Town Hall, a large Recreational Centre that contained a full basketball court, a stage with banks of lights and a state-of-the-art sound system was built.

Also caught in the glow of gold, the Episcopalian dynasty of the Yukon built a church and a residence for the pastor and his family, the likes of which rivalled structures in Carson City Nevada. The church even had a steeple and a brass bell that came over the mountains, pulled all the way from Whitehorse by a team of horses in an empty ore truck.

All of the early buildings had a certain confident majesty built with truckloads of bricks shipped over the high mountain divide to build "proper" structures rather than locally hand-sawn lumber. Instead, the timber that came was all imported from the big spruce mills down south; giving the

Village a majestic character reflecting the dreams of the occupants. And when the seam was wide and the gold company confident of what the future held, elegance and substance were the guiding dreams for the community. The church, for example, was envisioned to eventually be a "Cathedral." The large Town Hall had a Courtroom, with Judge's Chambers and a short-term jail to accommodate lawbreakers, until a Judge who periodically would come over from Whitehorse to try cases and go fishing (not in that order). Since there were very few cases, the judge spent most of his time fishing.

To accommodate the rapidly growing number of cases of "Black Lung Disease" in the miners, there was soon a graveyard set above Town with a spectacular view.

Adjacent the graveyard there was a municipal meat storage house for keeping wild game for town residents through the winter.

The view from the Town of Lone Bull was breathtaking, overlooking the lake and a vast crown of glacier and snowcapped mountain-peaks that reached far out towards the Pacific.

Then suddenly, when the gold seemed that it would go on forever, it disappeared entirely! Exploring as hard as the company might, the seam was gone! Soon the gold company packed up their giant machines and left, leaving a residual community of ageing workers so enthralled with the mountains and the Lake, that they remained... most living on retirement cheques from the Company, from the Yukon Territory, and the Canadian government.

Below the Town of Lone Bull, on the shores of the vast lake named "Kolsana Lake", sat the ancient Indigenous Native village of K'weset. To the Tlingit Native peoples who lived there, K'weset meant "Source of Abundance." Fish, both freshwater trout, and salmon from the Pacific Ocean were the mainstays. But the Village also sat at the head of an inlet bay that caught the first sun of Spring though a breach in the crown of mountain peaks that circled the Lake. As a result moose, caribou and deer were drawn to the Natives' doorstep in the Spring to feed on the early vegetation at the edge of the receding snow.

But it was also named K'weset because it was, according to Tlingit legend, the Source of "Life" itself.

More-over the "Source of all Life to the World" because it was there that Raven dropped all Life on the Planet, en route to another system.

As the Tlingit Legend went, Raven was carrying "LIFE" to another place, but when HE saw the Lake and Valley surrounded by a ring of majestic mountains, He was so taken with the place, that he dropped His cargo at the Village's current location.

Isolated from the outside world, and gifted with an abundance of fish, wild game, flocks of transient birds, and rich black soil for planting abundant gardens in the Spring, the Village thrived and to tell their history they carved five totem poles to protect the Village. (Archaeologists dated the encampment by its totems to be over 500 years old.)

Also, isolated from the outside world from Whitehorse and the main Northern Highway connecting British Columbia to the south and Alaska to the North, the Native culture flourished without impact from non-Native outsiders who lived side by side with them without strife due to an essential need for sharing in the face of mutual hardships.

But there was little cross-border culture integration. Mainly from the Native's perspective, it was not from racial issues, but rather it was lack of interest on the Natives' part. Digging holes in the ground, or mountain in this case, and crawling into them, seemed absurd. Unfortunately for them, the arrival of the outsiders triggered beyond their culture a dark chapter when the youth left for the outsider's World and soon became ensnared by addictions; by alcohol, lipstick and model magazines, snowmobiles and all too often Hollywood films in which they were portrayed as 'bad guys' bent on burning and scalping.

Some came back with addictions. Too often some came back in coffins and body-bags. But most, realizing that they already had what they were looking for, returned to stay.

. When a non-local, non-Native showed up in K'weset, everyone got nervous like chickens with a fox in the area. Stemming from a long history of being duped out of any benefits off their land by giant land altering ideas, yet left with the aftermath, presumably forever.

Unfortunately, a new proposal had recently emerged. The "Yukon Territorial Energy Commission" The electrical energy wing of the Territorial Government, wanted to dam the Lake and raise its elevation twenty meters to generate more electricity for the Territory. The proposed dam would flood the entire K'weset Village and cover all five ancient totem poles!

The Native's defence was simply... "It is a Sacred Site. That's why we live here."

But in a court of "Outsider's" law, "Sacred Site" was not in the Government's vocabulary. However, in exchange for any loss or inconvenience, the Yukon Government offered to relocate the Natives further up the mountain to the civilized facilities at Lone Bull and re-house them in "brand-new" trailers, complete with cable television with access to fifty channels!

The people of K'weset refused.

After serious consideration, an alternative was presented to the Yukon Territorial Government and the People of Lone Bull.

"We the Tlingit Nation and residents of K'weset do here-by give notice to the people of Lone Bull that we have decided to expand the Valley's airport which is upon our land."

"Therefore, as is our right by multiple treaties, drafted and signed by both Territorial and the Tlingit Nation; we hereby give notice to all residents of Lone Bull that you will have to seek

new residencies since the entire community of Lone Bull will sit directly in the flightpath of the new airport expansion. This will includc the removal of the Episcopal Church Steeple IMMEDIATELY!"

Because it was written by hand, on expensive, quality paper, framed with plenty of hang-on-the-wall certified credentials, and notarized by a respected lawyer and imprinted with an official looking embossed stamp, reading 'Office of the Tlingit Nation', further discussion of the Hydro Electric dam was terminated.

Chapter 1

Maktu leaned against the porch rail as the razor thin rays of winter dawn caught the top tips of the surrounding mountain peaks. The air had substance as it shimmered with diamond-dust-ice-crystals and time hibernated on the edge of death, suspended in the silence that enveloped the valley. Life without sound, time without change. There are three tragedies in life, his Grandmother had told him. We can't see the future, change the past, or hold the moment. He accepted his past, cared little for the future beyond that day, but Maktu thought he could stay in that moment forever. Maktu was comfortable living alone in what others called "Wilderness". It was all he knew. His parents and two siblings, a younger sister and an older brother had died in a car accident when a drunk on the highway hit them head-on killing everyone, the driver was their cousin. Maktu had been left with his Grandparents who lived in K'ewanka, a remote, but once active Native village far away from the newer one the Yukon government constructed to bring the Native population closer to the Territorial schools. It was his Grandmother who taught him how to draw and paint, read and write in that order. On the rare occasions when they went out to an Anglo community, she would buy with money made selling furs, sketch pads and brushes, watercolours and sometimes even commercial artist oil paints. But the oils were expensive, and by chance she discovered at the dump, buckets of house paints with remnants left in them, and old tent canvases that no longer deflected the rain and snow but worked well holding oil paints.

Gifted in capturing the structural element of the wilderness that surrounded them, even moods and feelings of the wildlife, she realised he had an innate talent to encourage. And soon, as a teen, he was supplementing his Grandfather's trapping income by selling pictures of his wilderness. "Paint what you feel. Not just what you see, your cousin Kaya's camera can do that...Use what you feel, not just what you see" was his Grandmother's mantra.

Maktu was used to living away from human settlements. "Living in the bush" was the Anglo phrase for a place in the northern wilderness void of human impact or signatures. Maktu shivered, for even though the mountain peaks across the lake began to smoulder in the early dawn with sheets ablaze like wind-swept embers from a campfire, it was a new dawn for him, a new adventure. No, often an arctic inversion raced into the Valley, sending a surf of amber waves of snow blazing across the frozen lake's surface, but this time they heralded a new adventure for which he had no previous experience. He drank the last of the coffee and pitched the grounds across the snow in front of the cabin. No, he couldn't stay. He was out of food, out of paints and he was going to try something his Grandmother had encouraged him to do. For the entire winter he had exclusively painted. His Grandmother had encouraged him to do what was his gift, and that was paint. He'd taken a few small paintings and shown them to an Art Gallery in Whitehorse and to encourage him they sold him more art supplies at cost. Surprisingly, the two large canvases that were on display at the Yukon Hotel and the one at the Airport also sold, and both places encouraged him, and provided him with enough money to allow him to buy the full cache for the winter supplies which, in conjunction with the pelts from the previous winter of trapping gave him enough money to buy the survival supplies plus enough for him to produce a total of forty canvases!

But it was time to leave, he was out of food. The caribou he'd shot and smoked that fall was down to a few bones which he shared with his dog Shag, and for vegetables he was reduced to potato skins which he also shared with Shag. Though Saint Bernard was likely his dominant lineage, Maktu suspected somewhere in his lineage there was a wolf. Mainly black with islands of white scattered across his landscape, his colour alone had saved Maktu's life. The occasion was the previous year when in a low cloud whiteout, Maktu's snowmobile and sled had broken through a weak ice crust, Chris, from the air spotted the black dog and was able to hoist the machine out of the fractured lake!

Maktu waited for Chris until mid-morning without any radio contact which was not uncommon since Chris owned and flew the only helicopter West of Whitehorse and therefore was accustomed to having to fly into remote places in the wilderness on emergencies. Problem births, life threatening chainsaw injuries; Chris was the ambulance service for the entire Northwest, which was in keeping with his early helicopter training in Vietnam where he had to rescue men severely wounded or pinned downed under gunfire, or both.

With a sigh Maktu rose from his porch chair and ducked under the door frame's cross beam as he entered the cabin, causing his long black hair to fall beside his face like blinders.

Over the years the rafters were becoming increasingly low as the foundational logs resting on the ground were slowly rotting down. He would definitely have to sell some of this year's paintings to buy some concrete blocks and cement to put the cabin on a proper foundation. Maktu was a tall man, and he now had to squat significantly to see his face in the mirror. The art gallery in Whitehorse, that had shown his work had sold three of his paintings to an art gallery owner, a sport salmon fisherman from New York. And he had left him a card and a written note requesting contact to discuss more paintings and possibly a show. Maybe the gallery in New York would buy some of this winter's work and it would generate enough cash for a new foundation on the cabin.

Maktu had crafted a letter via Chris a few weeks earlier to the Sullivan Gallery saying that he had had a good winter and that he had well over three dozen paintings of various sizes finished and he would bring them out to Lone Bull and would send pictures to the address that the pilot Chris had given him.

When Chris hadn't radioed to Maktu by 8:00am, Maktu assumed that an emergency had called him to respond, so Maktu took the load of paintings and a duffel of summer clothes down to the dock; hooked the cargo sled to the snowmobile and lashed everything... the duffel and particularly the paintings carefully onto the sled. He called to Shag, made a nest on top of the load for the dog in case the snow turned soft and wore Shag out from running behind the machine. Even if Chris was just delayed and came down the lake later, he would see them out there and could land on the helicopters skids and pick them up.

Returning to the cabin, he went inside, bent over in front of the mirror, corralled his hair into a ponytail, and went to tie it with an elastic band, but the rubber snapped with the cold. He took a leather thong from a nearby nail and tied his hair with it.

His pack frame lay on the bunk empty like collapsed parachute. There were only a few things to fill it with; his bedroll, a change of clothes, his paintbrushes, a couple meals of caribou jerky, and a small loaf of bannock he'd baked the night before. Besides, he laughed, he could always eat some of the dog's food which was the last few caribou ribs – though he'd cooked his serving. His paintings had been carefully packed separately from each other and wrapped in their own waterproof bags and then re-wrapped in another heavy waterproof canvas bag.

Putting on his parka and his fur hat, he did a final inventory of the cabin and satisfied himself he had everything ready for the trip out. There was no reason to stay. Besides, Chris was scheduled to fly down early that morning to pick him up, but as often happened with Chris, he was called elsewhere by some emergency. Chris would see his tracks.

Also, with the sudden warm snap following a winter of sub-zero temperatures, punctuated by trees rupturing, and splitting open with the 'bang' of a rifle, it was definitely time to leave while he could. It was a welcome relief knowing Spring was beginning. But it was also a forewarning of the pending most dangerous time... avalanche season! Suddenly the cornices would collapse under their own weight, and due to just a few degrees of rising temperature, they'd turn the faces of mountains into death zones.

That is what had happened just that morning. A giant cornice cemented onto the mountain, suddenly had exploded sending thousands of tons of snow and ice thundering down into the Valley with such force that just their sound and power triggered others until all of the mountains surrounding the Lake released their loads. Hopefully, the Lake itself would still have enough crust that he could make the run into Lone Bull without a problem. If he took a route due North and close to the Hankin Range, he could reach Lone Bull by evening.

Taking his pack, skis and poles down to the Lake, he carefully finished packing the cargo sleigh making a cocoon in the top of the stack of his canvases, then balancing the rest of the weight front to back on either side, he covered the load with a canvas tarp. Maktu knew Shag would eventually tire and would have to ride. Also, just in case things didn't go as planned, he tied his skis and poles onto the side of the cargo sled.

Finally, he left a note for Chris in a can marked with flagging tape on the porch of his cabin. At last, he turned for a nostalgic moment.... it was time to leave.

An arctic cold front had flushed through, followed by a Spring thaw of warm weather that had settled in fast, and at last, he no longer heard the rifle-reports of pine trees, checking and rupturing in the once frozen forest that lined the lake shore.

At first, the snow was hard and fast, and Shag galloped beside the snow machine, but by mid-morning it grew warm with the full sun and Shag started breaking through and lagging behind, and finally he had to ride on the sled behind the snowmobile until they reached the off-shore, windswept crust where he could easily run again.

Maktu assumed that either a medical crisis or bad weather had kept Chris from meeting him but the blizzard from the night before had now broken and still the helicopter hadn't arrived. The high alpine, because of avalanches would be impossible to cross this time of year, he would have to follow the lake, and to avoid breaking trail through the new avalanche chutes.

Midday and midway up the Lake towards Lone Bull, Maktu stopped and studying the effects of the vast chorus of early morning avalanches, he saw that one seemed to run down the ridge where the miner McLeod had his tunnel mine and cabin. He was making good time, so Maktu decided to take a detour and check on the miner.

McLeod lived on an arm of the Lake that ran a little way to the North. As Maktu approached he also saw that the shoreline was shattered, presumably by the massive chain of avalanches that had run throughout the Valley early that morning, forcing him to negotiate through the fractured shore-ice until he came to McLeod's. He noticed just to the West, a channel, and possibly another avalanche had swept down the ridge near McLeod's mine shaft.

Leaving his snowmobile and tow-sled on the shore he approached McLeod's cabin with Shag on his heals

"McLeod!" He called, but no answer. There were snow-laced

boot tracks going in but none coming out. The miner must be inside and Maktu started to knock again when he heard the unmistakable sound of a lever-action chambering a bullet into a carbine rifle. He jumped to the side of the door and the protection of the log wall.

"You stupid son of a bitch." He muttered under his breath.

"McLeod! It's me Maktu, your neighbour down the Lake, put the fuck'n gun down."

"Maktu?" The words were slow in coming.

"Yah, Maktu from down the lake. Are you hurt?" He heard a faint groan and reached for the door, turned the handle, moved to the side before thrusting the door open.

Even in the dark room he saw the figure slumped forward against a post – the gun hanging listless in his hand. Slowly it slumped forward. Maktu grabbed him and shuffled him to a chair by the table. In the light of the open door Maktu could see he was covered in blood; the source was his hands that were crimson and dripping blood on the floor.

"Holy Fuck!" Maktu swore. Quickly he looked around the room and found a dish towel and tore it into strips and tied both wrists to slow down the bleeding. He again scanned around the room and found a pan of water on the stove. The stove was warm but hadn't held fire for hours.

Immediately he built up the fire causing McLeod to scream. The heat, minimal as it was, was excruciating to the raw flesh. Maktu shut the damper and opened the cabin door for a few minutes.

Maktu then found a Coleman lantern, beside it a box of wooden matches on the table and lit it. The light suddenly revealed the full squalor of the miner's cabin. Maktu built up the fire in the Ashley stove and set a can of concentrated soup to heat which he found on a shelf above the table.

As soon as the stove began casting off heat, he stripped off the miner's heavy wet parka, his wool pants and shirt; and wrapped him with a blanket off the bed. Beneath the bed he discovered a box of clothes, filthy but dry. Soon the soup can was hot, Maktu cut a wedge through the soup's lid and poured the contents into a bowl and threw in a handful of snow to dilute it.

The miner started to be human again as he licked the last drops of soup out of a bowl. Maktu took down the miner's tobacco tin and rolled himself a smoke. He then filled a pan with snow and set it on the stove to melt so that he could wash away the blood on the miner's face and hands.

The inside of the cabin betrayed much about its occupant. By the door hung wool pants, heavy coveralls covered with a paste of drill dust, beside them was a dented miner's helmet. Beneath them on the floor, there was a case of 20% dynamite and a package of detonator caps.

The bed was simply four poplar posts supporting a 2x4 frame that held a sheet of plywood and a bedroll. A sock draped from one of the bed posts. On the wall above the bed was a Playboy centrefold and another rifle, both had seen better times. The stove was in the centre of the room with wires tied from the chimney to the different quadrants, making a spider's web of clothes drying lines. There was only one window in the cabin, at the front of the building towards the lake. In it there were four small panes, each of which were sealed in a thick grease and smoke covering.

On the windowsill lay some rifle cartridges and some dead flies probably from the last summer. Beneath the window was a table permanently anchored onto the building. The only piece of movable furniture was a wooden bench. On the table sat an open tin of tobacco, a paper container of "When It Rains It Pours " salt, a large tin of pepper, a half dozen Zane Grey novels. One of which was open face down. Also, there was a hand painted portrait of McLeod that Maktu had done. Beside it there was a half-played game of cribbage. Probably started when Chris was last there with supplies. Chris and Maktu were likely the only ties the miner had anymore with humanity.

He could trace the miner's daily routine by the scrubbed traffic trail in the thick soot that covered every surface in the log structure. Against the logs by the door there were tracks where he had leaned taking off his boots. McLeod was a big man as evidenced by the wear on the ceiling where he had rubbed his head. From door to stove, to table, to the bed, the paths were well established, the pattern was followed diligently like a monk working off a penance. Maktu traced the trail out to the wood porch and back to the stove.

"Oh, sweet Jesus!" Maktu gasped when he saw clearly the miner's hands once more. Blood still continued to drip from the ends of the fingers, bones protruded from the frozen flesh. Maktu reached to take his hands and suddenly the miner recoiled as if seeing Maktu for the first time.

"McLeod?" He yelled at the figure, but the man made no response... at least one that was human. Still like a frightened animal, he coiled ready to run or charge

"McLeod, it's Maktu. Maktu, your friend. Don't you remember? We are friends. We know each other." It was like the previous few minutes hadn't happened. Maktu knew that he had to keep talking, forcing the miner to deal with a human voice, otherwise he was either going to bolt... or attack.

"Maktu the painter. Remember? I did that picture for you. Here," he picked the small portrait off the shelf, "here it is, remember?"

Cautiously Maktu leaned towards him, trying to get around McLeod to cut off his path for the door. "Look, it's you. A picture of you. You sat there at the table when I did it, remember?" Maktu held the painting in front of the man partially blocking his vision until he could catch the door with his foot and gently draw it closed.

"Maktu?" The voice sent shivers through Maktu. From lack of use it was the sound of a child unsure of itself and for a moment the madness passed from his eyes.

Then suddenly, McLeod grasped the gun again, waving it violently.

Maktu grabbed the man by the shoulders and turned him to the bench again and once again near the stove, the warm air made the blood run faster and there was a trail of it across the room that puddled by his sides. Maktu carried in wood to build up the fire.

"Aahhh!" screamed McLeod again. He held his hands before his face, his frozen fingers were starting to thaw. Maktu took the kettle of water from the stove filled it with snow and poured the water into a basin which he set on the table in front of McLeod. Careful not to touch the raw flesh and protruding bone ends, Maktu tried to bring the hands to the water, but the miner pulled them away. Their eyes locked.

"McLeod, it's alright. It's me, Maktu. Your friend." Slowly the giant paws relaxed and gave in to Maktu's pressure. The water turned crimson from the blood once more.

"Do you have any whiskey?"

The miner's eyes narrowed.

"No, I won't steal it. It will help the pain."

Maktu's words were slow to register on the miner, but finally he grunted, "Under the floor... trap door." He motioned his head towards a leather strap nailed to the flooring near the bed. Lifting it Maktu found a cache of empty bottles, a metal ammunition box and a half full gallon bottle of Navy Rum.

"Here, drink this." he poured some into a coffee cup and held it to the miner's lips. It was then that Maktu saw it. A large section of the man's face was deathly white from frostbite.

"What happened?" asked Maktu. Again, the words were slow to take hold. It was clearly the first time the miner had confronted himself with the previous events, Maktu guessed, that the man was still doing the "Moose Trot"... staying alive by instinct and animal rote. But finally, the man looked up to answer.

"Avalanche. ... mother fuckn' avalanche! It broke off from above. Must have jumped the barrier to my mine shaft." The sentences came slow and difficult. "Closed the fuck'n entrance to the mine." He raised his hands out of the basin. "Tried to dig out!"

They sat in silence for a while. Maktu poured another cup of the rum, held it for McLeod. "Has Chris been around?"

McLeod didn't respond. "Have you seen Chris?" He watched the miner's face for recognition.

"Jesus Christ!" He yelled. "Chris, the pilot. He brings you your supplies. Has he come here in the last few days?"

The anger of Maktu brought McLeod upright "No. Chris ain't here. Don't know where he is. Ain't seen him in weeks." Again, the two men sat alone with their thoughts. The rum freshened McLeod's numbed brain cells, and he brought his eyes to meet Maktu's. "Something's wrong?"

Maktu then noticed that the basin was again thick on the surface with coagulated blood. "Do you have any clean cloths? We'll have to wrap those fingers before you bleed to death." McLeod shook his head, no. "What about the First-Aid kit Chris gave you?"

"Let it be." McLeod snapped. "It don't matter no more." He held Maktu with a savage stare but then stopped in thought. "It's good you come; I want you to do something. Yes, I will need my hand fixed just this one." He held out his right hand.

"Sorry partner, I don't do singles. It's either both or none at all."

Reluctantly, the man consented. Maktu found the First Aid box stuffed far under the bed. It hadn't been opened since Chris first left it; the bandages were still fresh in their paper packets. Amazing that he didn't use them for toilet paper and drink the rubbing-alcohol, thought Maktu.

Also in the box was a notebook, actually a detailed diary. "I was born in Buck's county Tennessee. My Daddy worked for the Black Star Coal Company in the shafts. Died in that mine. Mother had five of us before she died, only 3 were Daddy's and the last two were by a Monkey Ward suit salesman. Never knew him. He took Ma and them what couldn't fare for themselves to Chester County. But I left before so I didn't pay no never mind. 'Cept I sure missed my sister Sadie. She and I could read each other like books."

'Seemed like no one else gave a rat's ass about us, sure not Henry. He used to beat me before I growed. When I hea'd the news that one of my brothers was dead in the cave-in of '36, I prayed to the God-almighty that it was Henry. But he didn't work that day and it was Raymond instead. He was the only good brother to my way of thinking. But I know'd right then that either there ain't a God, or He don't give a diddle-squat about us."

"What killed Henry? Too much religion! Too many..'jump-ups' to praise the Lord"

Suddenly McLeod swung his hands knocking over the bowl that Maktu used to clean the miner's raw fingers.

"Oh, sweet Jesus!" Maktu gasped when he saw his hands again. Blood was again dripping from the ends of his fingers, and the raw bones stuck out even more from the frozen flesh.

"McLeod?" Maktu yelled at the figure, but the man made no response... at least one that was human. Like a frightened animal, he coiled ready to run or charge

Maktu grabbed the man by the shoulders and moved him to the edge of the bed and eased him down. The warming room from the stove made the blood gush more leaving a trail across the room.

"Aahhh!" screamed McLeod. He held his hands before his face; his frozen fingers were starting to burn with a new level of pain!

It was then that Maktu saw that the Navy Rum bottle was empty.

"Do you have any more rum?"

The miner's eyes narrowed with suspicion.

"No, I told you, I won't steal it. It will help the pain."

Maktu's words were slow to register but finally the miner grunted, "More under the floor." He motioned his head towards a leather strap nailed to the flooring near the bed.

Lifting the strap once again Maktu found the metal ammunition box, but as he rummaged around further though the pile of empty bottles, he did find a half full gallon bottle of Navy Rum.

Maktu realised that the miner had made his decision and no matter what Maktu did to change that, the man was resigned to die!

Also, he realised, that the longer Maktu waited to make his move to Lone Bull, the greater the odds that he too might die on the trail. No, he had to go, and even then, he would have to drive in the dark by the lights on the snowmobile.

"McLeod. I'm leaving."

"Hey Injun," bellowed McLeod as Maktu reached the door. "Fetch that steel box from under the floor. And keep your eyes peeled for any more rum. Too bad Chris ain't around he'd bring me some more!".

McLeod said nothing more, only stared at Maktu as he moved to the door.

Shag leapt to his feet as Maktu came out of the cabin. Then suddenly from inside came again the voice of McLeod.

"Hey come back! I told you to look again in the trap, there's an envelope! Take it to Brand, the lawyer. Give it to him... you hear Indian? Give it to only him!"

Maktu found the manilla envelope. He didn't open it, only glancing at it as he put it inside his parka's inner pocket. It had the lawyer's name on it.

"Goodbye you dumb son-of-bitch!"

Maktu motioned for Shag to lay down in the nest for the dog that he had made on the top of the cargo sled. He then put a collar on him and snapped it to a rope-tie on the sled's side-rail to keep Shag from being thrown off. He knew the last leg was going to be completely in the dark and illuminated exclusively with the snowmobile's front headlight.

As the machine droned across the frozen lake, Maktu thought about the events that pulled McLeod into his self-imposed isolation.

The story he knew was that back when the Lone Bull mine was still running, McLeod was a hard rock miner in the main shaft of the Lone Bull mine. When the ore body suddenly stopped and most of the crew followed the company moving to another property far away to the south in British Columbia, McLeod remained. He had a theory that given the abrupt end of the gold vein, the mountain had shifted and that he could pick it up on the other side and hence he found a likely spot on the other side of the mountain, staked it and proceeded to dig into the mountain.

Loneliness brought him into Town and at a church social in

the dead of winter he met one of the schoolteachers, Joedean a lonely woman herself from Tennessee intent to find a "real man". They courted for nearly a year until finally, with Winter going full throttle and isolation holding the human psyche by a thin thread, and, with the breaking up of the ice on the rivers giving fuel to the human mind to do the same, McLeod decided it was time to propose. But not before he had a shot of courage at his friend Johnny Coldwell's house.

Johnny was in fact having a "snort" with George Jayton and reasoning a second drink would increase his courage and tonal qualities, McLeod, when he left his friends, was full of courage. And with resolve, outside her door he turned his bravado into song.

Unfortunately, where he planted himself, was both downwind and out of sight from the object of his passion, and the louder he sang the more she concluded that the storm was swelling. McLeod, crushed by her lack of response, slunk away and found refuge in the town's garage that housed the community's D4 bulldozer.

It took five grown men, and an animal tranquilliser gun to stop him, but not before he crashed through the double doors of the garage, two of the community's street light standards, and a kid's bicycle that was left in a snowdrift in the fall, and a significant section of the Village's church.

Having no previous criminal record the judge ruled insanity due to cabin-fever and winter-madness, and $340 in fines.

It was dark when Maktu turned the corner of the Lake and the lights of K'weset and Lone Bull on the ridge above, came into view. There was one dominate light-standard on the dock that became his target.

Slowly the lights became distinct, and he aimed for the one dock with a boat ramp he could drive onto. Then suddenly before he could react, he saw that the avalanches from the morning, had crashed into the lake, turning the shore-ice into a wall of upthrust slabs. Jerking off his left glove he grabbed his knife out of his hip scabbard, and cut Shag's tether to the sled and snow machine and then the one he'd tied around himself!

He downthrottled... but it was too late! The snowmobile crashed into an upthrust slab, flipping it sideways and it sunk into the frozen water... pulling the cargo sled with it – throwing Maktu and Shag into the freezing water!

Chapter 2

Dear Kay,

It has been a very long time since I wrote. So much has happened! When I last corresponded, I broke up with Thomas ... when he asked me to marry him. My parents were horrified that I should not marry a blossoming doctor when I had just finished my advanced nursing degree. To tell you honestly, it was not Daniel, in fact he was a flawless, promising young doctor, taking over his father's practice, etc.

Alas, I wanted something more exciting, more unpredictable. Some place new, exciting!

The first "boom of an explosion!" outside was definitely something hard hitting the cabin door and not just a gust from the blizzard that had suddenly come up in the evening. Possibly it was another piece of the wooden sled runner from her distant neighbour, the Loechild family. His up-ended dog sled was slowly coming apart as his puppy chewed away the caribou-sinew webbing that held it together.

The second noise was certainly a dog howling followed by what was clearly not an errant piece of the dog sled and the accompanying moan made her blood run cold... and it didn't ease in the ensuing silence.

"Who is it?" She stopped typing and called out. Again silence.

As it grew, her thoughts raced to the worse and she looked to the gun loaded with grizzly slugs against the wall not far from the bed.

"Who is it?" She called again above the wail of the winter storm.

Just as she reached for the 12-gauge shotgun, her answer came – the anxious bark of a dog, a domestic dog in distress.

She rushed to the door leaving the rifle alone. As soon as she released the dead bolt, the wind and the weight of a body leaning against it, threw the door open wide!

The fifty below air sucked the breath from her lungs, and burned like acid on her bare skin, and she leapt back in horror, letting a body fall into the room. If anything, it was more a body than a living human. When it did not move, she grabbed his legs relying on a history of slinging calves around on her parents Saskatchewan farm, and she pulled him into the room and slammed the door.

It took a moment to grasp the situation. It was human. A man and he was clearly in hypothermic shock – if not dead already. His clothes had been soaking wet at some time and had frozen against his skin. Again, she heard the dog outside. "Oh my God!" She gasped and let him in immediately. He went directly to the body sniffing its length, licking its face. Finally, the dog turned, looked at the woman as if asking for her help and then, to the woman's astonishment, he went to the corner of the room at the end of the bed, and lay down watching them.

What she remembered was to heat the body cautiously!!! Then try raise it as soon as possible to 40 degrees centigrade.

She had to get his clothes off but they were frozen stiff. The fire had dwindled to a nightly minimal heat that would last throughout the night, but it was fully loaded with wood. Quickly, she closed the intake valve and changed the damper in the chimney to draw as much air as possible through the firebox.

Beginning with his fleece-skin cap, then mitts, there was only one and, jacket, slowly, cautiously she undressed him. His trousers were the hardest, the legs of the caribou hide leggings had frozen stiff like planks. But finally, she stripped him down to his long johns. She wanted to take it off with surgical exactness, the flesh underneath was likely severely frostbitten. She remembered her nursing instructor saying that when flesh is frozen, it is critical not to touch, just warm slowly otherwise you'll breakdown the cells. Her government-issue nursing kit had few tools, but it did have bandages and surgical scissors.

The fire caught up quickly, and the cabin soon warmed, and then turned hot, painfully hot for the man and he started to moan though his fetal form was still rigidly twisted. For a moment the woman considered opening the door a crack to cool the cabin down, but the wail of the building blizzard stopped her. The floor was still cold, and the woman turned down the airflow to the stove's firebox.

Her mind raced to her nurse's training. Carefully dry and SLOWLY begin the warming process half a degree to 2 degrees/hour. Insulate the body to prevent further heat loss, OR too much heat would do damage as well. She was at a loss. The floor was bitter cold, and she could never get him onto the bed.

Her mind raced for ways she might bring up his body-temperature without overheating it. Suddenly she hit upon a solution. It was definitely unorthodox, but she was at a loss. The one thing that she had from the Yukon Government which she hoped she'd never use, was a body bag. For not only was she the village nurse, and teacher; she was the also the 'Assistant Coroner' ... in that she had a telephone number for the real coroner in Whitehorse – plus a body bag to hold corpses until a plane could bring in a professional. If she could insulate it with both blankets inside and under it outside, strip down the body, dry it and get it inside the body bag, it's own heat would do much to regulate changes in his body temperature.

But that was just an emergency short term solution. She needed help, professional help but the nearest hospital was in Whitehorse.

Cautious not to touch him, she laid out the body bag and opened it beside him. The dog had a troubled look when she opened the window a crack on the "out of the wind" side of her cabin and began scooping snow out of the near wind-bank with a cooking pot and dumping it along the body bag. She considered cutting off the man's underwear but felt it might soften the shock of the cold snow and hopefully protect his skin in the process of warming up plus slow down the rate of warming. She needed help.

Because it was late at night there was no traffic on the short-wave radio, and she was able to get through to an operator on night shift at the Whitehorse Hospital who immediately transferred Christina to the Doctor on Emergency. Taking a deep breath to calm herself she explained the situation

"Bring him in IMMEDIATELY!" the doctor advised, then fell silent when he heard the full breadth of the situation.

"OK. We'll have to get him over the Pass in the morning – your airstrip has no emergency landing lights." He said rhetorically. "Besides, your resident pilot at the Lone Bull strip isn't responding."

"FUCK!" Christine exclaimed uncharacteristically. She knew Chris and flying at night in the dead of Winter was almost commonplace for him, but missing 'in action' was a different matter. Something was definitely wrong!

"OK." The doctor said. "So, here is the textbook procedure for hypothermia. Get him out of his wet clothes. Dry him off, if possible, and rewarm up the body slowly... half a degree to 2 degrees per minute".

She explained she had no dry clothes that would fit him, but she told him about the idea of lining a body bag with blankets, stripping off the wet clothes and manoeuvring the man into it.

"Brilliant!" Said the doctor. "Can you get warm drinks into him... that will help considerably. Remember to do everything in gradual portions, his body is probably in a state of severe shock."

Christina realised it meant cooling down the cabin, so she damped down the stove a little and put on her heavy down-parka, wool pants, socks and gloves.

"I've just learned," the doctor came back on the radio. "There is no one at your airstrip to turn on the landing lights or clear the strip of snow so you'll have follow the procedure I've outlined until morning... can you do that? I will send you a snow machine or a plane on Skis over with the dawn if we can't get through".

She laughed to herself. "Guess I don't have much choice, do I?" she said with resignation. "I'll try."

Once in the bag, the man's moaning decreased slightly but he showed no other signs of consciousness. When the moaning stopped all together, she feared he had died and was greatly relieved when a pain- wrenched sound began again from him. Taking the bandage scissors, she cautiously but quickly cut his underwear from his skin.

For some time, he lay in the body bag zipped up. She prodded the side of the bag lightly as a cook might test a thawing turkey. Finally, she unzipped the bag and cautiously, so as not to touch him, she dipped out the melted water and lightly dried him with towels and a sleeping bag as best as she could. Then taking the body bag by the top handle she dragged bag and body to the side of her bed.

She encouraged him with words and gentle pressure to get him to move, hopefully onto the bed but it wasn't possible, so she put the mattress onto the floor.

The man's scream was horrifying and would be tattooed forever into her memory, but she knew before she began that it was one of those situations where once started, it had to be carried through without reservation. With him screaming even more, she manhandled him more quickly, even violently, onto the mattress and straightened out his body as best she could.

Though his scream masked even the howl of the storm – it was more frightening when he suddenly he fell silent, unconscious. But the effort of getting him onto the mattress, and pain from doing it caused his body to start shaking, and soon it escalated into violent convulsions. She covered him with two quilts, but the tremors did not stop. Quickly she stripped off her flannel nightgown and lay her body against his.

Talking to him like a mother would to a frightened child, or a child to an injured pet, she spoke with comfort and reassurance, all the while, silently, even unknowingly, pleading to something higher to intercede.

Suddenly at dawn there was a knock on the door. The cabin was no longer warm, but it was not freezing.

"Teacher Christina." A Native voice called out. It was Delbert Johnny one of the Native volunteer firemen. "You got a man in there?" It was more teasing than accusatory.

Cautiously they lifted the body bag, wrapped it in quilts and moved it into the rear seat of the Village's Bombardier snow packer. The door slammed, and the two men from the Village waved as the giant machine turned towards the airstrip.

Within an hour, in the first rays of day, she heard a plane. Relieved she turned back into the cabin and the man's dog, who was obviously confused by his master's absence and he whined and scratched at the door..

"It is going to be alright'". She said petting him, but she was not convinced herself.

"Oh my God!" She suddenly gasped and laughed when she looked at her computer. There on the screen was the email, she had last written before the bang at the door, the dog howling and the half-frozen man on her doorstep.

"There's nothing exciting here in my life!" She had just written.

"Oh my God!" She repeated to herself, putting her hands on the keyboard.

"Since this previous sentence a series of events of such significance have transpired that it feels like..." She hesitated to go on. *"they've changed my entire life! – BUT I don't know how or why!"*

With that, she proceeded to write her friend about the 'thump' on her doorstep, the howling dog, the half dead man, her attempts to save his life, the body bag, then finally the snow machine arriving to take him to the airport and the flight to the Whitehorse Hospital.

"The irony is, I don't know who the man is. I think he is a loner who lives far down the Lake by himself and that he makes his living painting pictures of the North. I've seen a few of his paintings in Whitehorse and when they are not for sale, but they are fabulous! And I'm told, when they are for sale, they command very high prices. I thought of buying one, but I couldn't afford it. There is one in the dining room in the Yukoner Hotel ... a very expensive hotel in Whitehorse. And as I remember, the painting was large and spectacular... and.. as said, not for sale!

I'm told the Legislature Building in Whitehorse has two of his pieces that are also very large and also not for sale. Imagine, I just saved the life of a Rembrandt. I still have his dog who has moved in, presumably until his master returns. All very strange!

And.... I was just whining about how boring my life is. I fear that has just changed.

I'll keep you informed,

Your loving friend,

Christina

Chapter 3

Christina sent the email to Kay, then looked around the cabin with disbelief. Where just hours before it was boringly organised, now it was complete chaos! For a woman who prided herself for being fastidious, suddenly her life was in chaotic shock! Order... she would be fine with 'order' and immediately she started making the cabin as it was before she opened her door and the man fell into her cabin. Her response was textbook for hypothermic shock, but still she felt there was more she could have done. Maybe it was because his dog was still in the cabin laying near the door, whining.

As she straightened the cabin and hung the man's clothes to dry on a line she'd strung in the cabin, she found a manilla envelope addressed to Brand (care of) the Lone Bull general store. It was from the miner she'd heard about who lived far down the lake. She needed groceries so at lunch she'd go into Town and drop it off with Mr. Chance.

On her way to school that morning she passed by the concrete dock on the lake and the scene where Maktu had collided with the upthrust slabs of shore ice. A backhoe was there and with chains lifting Maktu's snowmobile out of the fractured lake. The back end of the machine had been torn off; there was no sign of the cargo shed it likely pulled. Heavily loaded, it certainly had sunk to the bottom of the Lake which was very deep having been excavated to accommodate the haul boats.

At the school lunch break, Christina walked up to Lone Bull to get groceries and deliver the manilla envelope to Chance at the General Store.

All morning since Christina had dropped off the Will, Chance had been thinking about it. Likely it was the delusion of another 'Bushkin', as he called people, usually male outsiders who had come alone into the wild with a secret quest that there was someone that cared on the outside who would embrace them once they struck it rich... and returned, which they never did.

At midday, Chance turned over the General Store to his wife who normally in the morning did the book-keeping and he went up the street to see Brand about the Will.

"Do you recognise this?" Asked Chance, handing the Will over to the lawyer.

Gordon looked at it and knew it immediately. "So that crazy hermit miner finally died!" He nodded and handed the paper back to Chance.

Both men fell silent considering the ramifications of the Will, if McLeod had in fact, hit the back end of the original Lone Bull gold seam.

"I remember it well!" Brand reflected, "A couple of years ago McLeod came into the office to see me about drafting a Will. The strange thing is, he wanted to leave his possessions and his mining claim to the people of the Valley... Lone Bull, K'weset and the Landers."

"But I wasn't going to do it for free! And as I remember he stomped out the door, and I thought that would be the end of it. But no, when he came back to collect the Will, he did pay me.... and according to my books... he paid in gold."

"Back then, we had just immigrated to the Valley, and I thought that gold was normal for settling debts. ... this being a mining town and all."

The lawyer looked at Chance. "You remember, back then it was a time when mandatory conscription and the Vietnam War had brought a lot of us from the U.S. to northern Canada to avoid the draft... plus, we were seeking a new way of life."

Brand paused, then laughed. "Soon the parking lot outside of town was filled with abandoned Volkswagen campers as the refugees, like Martha and I, explored, and eventually settled, wild undeeded land at the far end of the Lake to build from scratch, self-sufficient farms with sustaining gardens and log homes."

"When the War ended, most of us stayed and our families grew, but the memories for what we'd left behind, plus our children coming of age, many of us returned to urban society and a formal education for our children." Brand smiled.

"But for me, I wanted a profession and went back for a degree in Law. Still, once I graduated from Law School, we returned to the Valley."

At the time Gordon thought it just another lone prospector's delusion. That his time in the bush should have social significance since the beneficiary of his mineral holdings was the inhabitants of the Valley including not just Lone Bull, K'weset but all of the residents on the lake which was basically just Maktu and the back-to the Landers down at the far end.

"By the fact that McLeod gave the Will to Maktu to deliver, I'd assume he saw his end was nigh." Said Chance. "I'm also guessing that yesterday's series of avalanches may have sealed off the entrance of his mine."

"Too bad Maktu isn't around for an update. But I am guessing that since McLeod gave him the Will to deliver that he wasn't planning on an extended future." "How is Maktu? I heard from the nurse Christina down at the K'weset Dock that he crashed coming in late last night and near froze to death. His dog dragged him to her cabin, and she arranged for him to be flown to Whitehorse by plane at dawn."

"Incredible." Brand shook his head. "Also, I just heard that Chris is "Missing in Action"... Is that right?"

"That's what I heard. I'm told he hasn't been seen since yesterday morning when he took off from the airstrip at dawn." Chance said. "That's probably why Maktu was coming out on his snowmobile."

For a long time both men were silent. "No one on the two-way radio has heard from Chris either?"

Silence filled the room.

"Ok. We have to treat this as what it seems," Brand said. "I don't think McLeod would have given the Will to Maktu if he didn't think the end was nigh."

Chance nodded in agreement.

"But" Brand continued, "The one contingent that he was emphatic about was that the bequest of the mine was contingent upon a "proper" burial in the Lone Bull cemetery and that his name be carved on a headstone!".

Both men looked at the other...both realising at the same time there was a problem – the ground at the cemetery was frozen solid for at least four feet down! And ..it would be another three months before it thawed!

After a contemplative silence, Chance spoke. "Maybe we're getting too far ahead. Maybe he's still alive. I got the Will from Christina the nurse and she from Maktu who has been taken to the hospital in Whitehorse."

"So, maybe we should go down to McLeod's and check on him." Gordon said finally. "But... my friend, we have both become townies and we have but one snow machine and one sled between us. If McLeod is in need of help the three of us won't be able to come out."

“Since tomorrow is Saturday,” said Chance. “And the Store is only open half day. Mabel could do the morning shift, and we could go down and check in on him then. The Fenton boys have that big snowmobile and that large cargo sled. If they are in accord, they could come down with us with that sled and if there is a body, we can haul it out on it.”

“Yes, that’s my thinking too that we should recruit the Fenton Brothers to come down with us on their big “Traveller’s” machine and bring the big cargo sled for McLeod if necessary.”

“You’re right.” conceded Chance. “I’ll go see the Fenton Brothers and see if they would be willing to go with us on the big snowmobile and the Traveller’s sled.”

Crank was in his shop working on a water pump that had frozen during a power outage in the last cold snap. Brand and Chance explained the situation and their request for him to accompany them down to McLeod’s with the large snowmobile and sled down Lake in case he’d died, and they had to retrieve the body. They didn’t mention the Will.

It would just be him, Crank. Unfortunately, ‘Smooth’ Fenton had taken the backhoe up the pass to start opening the road over it to Whitehorse, that had been closed by the avalanches the day before. But he glanced at the water pump, he’d love an excuse to get out of the shop and the snowmobile was fully gassed... he was in.

Chapter 4

The Fenton brothers were never miners, rather they were the Valley's heavy equipment operators and mechanics. And Lone Bull was never their destination, yet they remained, and so it was the Fenton brothers, Ernie and Benton, or as they would be nicknamed into the community 'Crank', the mechanic and 'Smooth', the operator were the glue that kept the villages running.

They came from a working farm in Alberta and therefore were hands-on familiar with both heavy equipment, long days in the summer and short, dark days in the Winter.

Where the difference showed between the two brothers was when something broke down. Earnie nicknamed 'Smooth' looked for the cause, and Benton, known as 'Crank', would fix it.

Smooth, the more thoughtful of the two brothers believed that hard work in a black hole underground, even in the pursuit of gold was ridiculous when a person could drive machines by the light of day instead of moving underground discharge in the dark of night. When the mine died, he became the town's equipment driver.

Smooth, the oldest of the brothers, a nickname he earned by leaving, after he ploughed or graded, a singularly flat surface. He was also held in high regard in the community because he got up at 4:00a.m. even at -52 degrees, he would put a tiger torch in an elbow of stovepipe, slide it under the oil pan of the town's D-6 bulldozer, so by 6:00 a.m., he could start the engine and plough main street to its end at the small hydro dam which powered the generator and then start it by 8:00 am for the village's injection of electricity.

His brother named 'Crank' not because of his disposition (in fact he was a gentle, easy-going man and happy to be inside a warm building in the winter and summer), was the town's mechanic.

Crank shared his brother's aversion for underground mining, and as a consequence he became the shop-bound mechanic for both Lone Bull and K'weset. From chainsaws to heavy equipment, Crank was the communities' engine repair man for the Towns' three pieces of heavy equipment, a backhoe, a D6 bulldozer, and the year-round road-grader. His job description further included repairing lighter motors such as snow blowers and lawnmowers... though there were only two parcels of lawn grass requiring mowing... the lawn at the Town Hall, including the Community Centre, and the graveyard located on a wide plateau above town.

Both brothers' wives were sisters, the daughters of the Episcopalian Minister. Actually, the huge Church was used by all undenominational faiths so whoever needed a pulpit could have one. As a consequence, it was a place of worship for many denominations, Lutheran, Catholic, Episcopal. but mainly Bingo. The cathedral structure was designed for a town of great projected wealth. It even had a bell on the steeple and a wind indicator that actually revolved with the wind at minus twenty degrees temperature.

Each of the Fenton brothers had not only married sisters, but they also lived beside each other. But you would not confuse the two-family dwellings. One house was a thick walled, prefabricated aluminium and geo-thermal house prefabricated in Edmonton –

that should last seventy years of hard winter winds.

The most distinguishable thing about Smooth's prefab modular house, however, was that the front yard was full of pink flamingos, (concrete statues on iron legs) which in the winter, when the snow was deep up to their bellies, the flamingos seemed to float on the surface of a frozen pond, as though they were on a lake in Florida. Thirty-two of them. And when the crust froze solid, a flock of ducks would move into the forests of flamingos whereby sheer numbers of the concrete figures, the ducks found sanctuary from the wolves and coyotes.

Secretly Smooth's wife also reasoned, because she bought the lawn ornaments through "Better Homes and Gardens,", the novelty of the flamingo story in the far Yukon North would make a marvellous promotion for the magazine's advertiser.

Bunny was a devout futurist so focused upon her convictions that Lone Bull would once again raise from the ashes, that she was blind to the current state of lethargic contentment that blanketed the community,

"Prosperity" and "Respect" were her icons that fuelled her dreams, even to those who said that if she were not so committed to her zealousness, she would see that she already had both. Still, she was respected for raising six well behaved children, each landing on their feet in the outside world, including two doctors, and having to deal with Smooth during his younger days.

The other brother, Crank's, home was a log-house. Singularly warm in the Winter, it retained the wood heat from a large Ashley 'Grandfather' stove that warmed the entire building for the full day with just one morning's loading.

The outside of Crank's yard was just the opposite of Smooth's. It was a jungle of northern spruce, pine, sage and willow without planned segregation or order. In the winter deer, moose, wolves and coyotes inhabited it.

Adjacent to the jungle of iron legged pink flamingos and concrete gnomes of their neighbours, there were wild rabbits. They were there not for natural food; in fact, they were fed with commercial rabbit food! No, the abundance of rabbits and small vermin was because they could easily hide from the coyotes, fox and wolves among the iron and concrete ornaments of the neighbour's.

When approached, the Fenton Brothers agreed that Crank would go with Brand and Chance, and provide their big snowmobile and a large, heavy-duty cargo sled called a "Traveller" if there was a body to retrieve. It was likely that McLeod had died already since he had given Maktu his Will or maybe he'd need help after the avalanches.

Chapter 5

It was a bright dawn morning when the three men in two snow machines travelled down the Lake to McLeod's cabin arriving just after noon. He was not there though there were tracks leading up towards the entrance to his mine. The avalanche had blocked the opening with tons of snow and debris, but Brand found a set of tracks that led up through the avalanche field, and they started to climb. The snow was so hard packed that snowshoes were unnecessary.

"Here he is!" Brand called out high above the entrance to the mine, but even up there, the slope was concrete hard with avalanche snow and debris from still higher above.

"And" he called down, "you're not going to believe this!" There was the body of McLeod holding, or more like wrapped around a huge spruce tree!

"He must have come up looking for an entrance into the mine, from above and when he found that the entire mountain was concrete hard with debris, he just gave up. We are going to have to get the body down to the Lake."

"More likely he triggered another slide and grabbed the tree for safety".

"Well, which ever, we can't leave him like this, and collect him in the Spring, the wolves and the vermin would certainly attack the body." Said Brand.

"We're going to have to fell the tree above him and somehow peel the body loose from the stump."

Dropping the tree above him went as planned. But immediately they saw that the next step to get the body free of the stump was going to be tricky as rigour mortis had compounded the freezing. And after considerable thought, it was decided to bring both the body and the section of the tree he had wrapped himself around, down the mountain and back to Lone Bull where it could be thawed and straightened as a unit.

On more than one occasion during the tedious and extremely arduous task of getting the body and the spruce chunk down the slope to the lake, they questioned that maybe it should be just left until Spring, and then come back and straighten it out. But it was Brand who pointed out the even in warm weather, rigour mortis would still concrete him into his embrace with the spruce.

No, they were going to have to bring the sled up from the snowmobile on the Lake, wrestle him and the chunk of spruce he embraced, onto it and then somehow get it down through the avalanche debris to the Lake.

It was dark when they finally reached the snowmobile on the Lake and got the cargo lashed down for the long and tedious run back to Lone Bull.

Fortunately, Brand had asked the Town Maintenance Man to leave the streetlights on so they could find Lone Bull and navigate the snowmobiles and sled through town. The question arose, "where to keep the body?"

Make a snowbank with the backhoe and stick it there was one suggestion... but the backhoe was up on the Pass clearing the road to Whitehorse. In the Mayor's garage was another suggestion but his truck was there on blocks for the winter. Finally, they hit upon a short-term solution, leave the body and stump in an empty storeroom in the back of the Store that Chance reserved for the winter wild meat. It was a weak solution since Chance didn't hunt and his wife was a vegetarian, but at 2:00 a.m.., it was good enough.

Chapter 6

Christina took the call at her school. It was the Whitehorse General Hospital, Doctor Moresby, Head of Surgery. After introducing himself, he explained the reason for the phone call.

"As you know Mr. Maktu was brought in with severe hypothermia, and specifically exposure of his left hand. We've put him in an induced coma for the last three days and the results should be very positive."

There was a long pause.

"But!" He said it with punctuation. "His left hand has been severely damaged from being directly exposed to the water and extreme sub-zero temperatures, resulting in hypothermic shock and lack of circulation..." There was a long pause. "I'm afraid gangrene has set in from being frozen and lack of circulation... and, we may have to amputate the whole hand!"

There was a long silence. "Can you tell me..." The doctor finally filled the void. "... what does he do for a living? Complete amputation may be our only choice!"

"OH MY GOD!" Exclaimed Christina. "He's an artist!! He's an oil on canvas painter!" There was a long pause of silence. "I believe a very well-known artist! In fact, he painted that large mural at the Whitehorse Airport! And I believe he also did the one in the entrance to the Hospital."

"DAMN!" The doctor exclaimed, followed by silence... "That's what I feared!" And again, a long silence on the phone.

"Why?" Christina asked.

"Judging by the calluses on his hands..."The doctor replied. "I think he is left-handed, and that's the hand that has been so severely damaged!"

Again, nothing was said for a long time. "I don't suppose there is any way I can reach his immediate family is there?"

"I've made many inquiries," said Christine... "and everyone knows him, but no one knows anything about him... not even his last name!"

This time the phone went quiet for so long that Christina looked to see if there was still a connection. But then, to her relief the Doctor came on again.

"So, here's the situation. I know we will have to take off two fingers on his left hand that are severely gangrenous, but I'm hopeful we can save the rest of his hand!"

There was silence, and then the doctor spoke as though talking with himself following a long session of weighing alternatives. "I'll try my best, that's all I can do!" Then suddenly he spoke once more before hanging up.

. "Oh! And by the way, the body-bag was ingenious! That alone probably saved his life!"

Chapter 7

"I have a job for you." Gordon smiled to his wife, "McLeod, in his Will, left his holdings... namely his mine to the people of Lone Bull and K'weset and the 'Down Lake Landers'. But how do you divide a mine equally? So, we think we've come up with a brilliant idea. We'll form a company and every person of age in the valley will be a member. And for their membership everyone gets a share in it."

"Basically, the idea is, we will print up a batch shares and distribute them equally to all of the residents of the Valley. Then, if there is ever any interest in the mine, we will all benefit equally."

She thought about it and cautiously embraced its merits. Still Nancy smiled, more out of indulgence than conviction.

"And..." He added cautiously, "Would you design them? They should look official and financially solvent so people will hang onto them in case someday the mine does prove to be valuable." He smiled. "And they have to look legal." Said Brand

Martha rolled her eyes.

"And will they be legal?"she asked.

"Of course!" her lawyer husband answered. "I think... maybe. I'll check!" He assured her.

"I can't wait to redeem them." She smiled. Still, she cleared her draft table and took out her pens and inks.

Two days later she turned out a very credible stock certificate, both sides with extremely ornate detailed scrolling so complex they couldn't be easily coped.

Written in an embossed frame was an intricate scrolled collage encircling the words:

*

ONE Redeemable SHARE

*** **THE LONE BULL BONANZA** ***

***

In the background there was a delicate but clear alpine floral imagery which she hoped would be difficult to counterfeit.

On the back of the share, a majestic bull caribou stood with huge antlers poised on a knoll in an alpine cirque surrounded by mountain peaks and a Valley far beyond and below in the distance.

Across the share's back was once again the message

One Redeemable SHARE

When Brand showed his wife's design of the McLeod Bonanza share to Chance, the shopkeeper was ecstatic.

"I'll take a high-definition photograph-copy of both sides and fax them over to the printer in Whitehorse for a quote. The hard part will be getting an appropriate fibre-paper."

Brand thought for a moment. "So, here's the deal. I've been doing some legal research, and it seems pretty straight forward. We form a legally registered company and make all the "Of legal Age" residents' equal members in it.

“At Council meeting tomorrow night I’ll introduce the idea and lay it all out. I think, with the equal share idea we shouldn’t have any problems getting the Council on board.”

“I think it is a great idea,” Said Chance. “But we don’t want to appear to be scamming mine promoters. Also, remember, nothing of nothing is nothing and we don’t want people to lose money in the transaction, The way I see it, it is a way residents can use their shares for beautiful looking wallpaper.”

“Doing the maths, I’d guess there are 250 legally registered, of-legal age, voters in the entire watershed. So, say we get a quote of 10 shares per person, that comes to a printing of 2,500 shares.

They were valued at $100/share and a quarter of a million total value for issuance of $1,000/per person with another 250 shares held in reserve.

“Is this legal?” Chance asked Brand.

“Probably not, but after all this is Lone Bull”.

“Which raises another question, can the shares be held by someone outside the Valley?”

“I can’t imagine anyone plunking down hard cash speculating on the potential wealth of a likely worthless hole in the ground. But why not, it’s done daily on the various Stock Exchanges. All you need is to induce someone who has a speculative attitude with deep pockets”.

Chance was apprehensive but he did have to admit that the shares artwork was certainly worth hanging on the wall, even though it could be worthless except as wallpaper.

Chapter 8

In the conference room, present was the Mayor's regular council plus Chance, Brand, and the Fentons since the four of them had some possible legal responsible for collecting the corpse. Also, both Betty and Sarah Tashoots attended representing the Native K'weset interests.

The Mayor spoke first. "The primary issue on the agenda is the body of McLeod and his Will."

"Now we all know that mine probably ain't worth the powder it'd take to blow it to Hell, especially since his soul is probably there already! But we have to cover all the 'what-ifs'. So, let's look at some rather startling facts!" He rolled out a set of geological topographic maps.

"Here is where the abandoned Lone Bull Mine sits, and here's the mine's entrance, the main shaft running at this angle before it peters out".

"Now," he said with enthusiasm and pulled out a second a sheet of topographic map, showing a side view of the lower mountain. "This here's the angle that the main shaft of McLeod's ran along. Now, if we draw a line between the main stem of the Lone Bull Mine to the McLeod tunnel from both of these maps, they intersect!"

"Well, I'll be a pink-assed whore!" Exclaimed Crank,

"That's right, but considerably lower, as if the mountain sheared in half and dropped." There was shocked silence in the room.

"Now I ain't saying that is the way it is, but I say let's considerate it!"

"Are you saying McLeod might have found more of the Lone Bull strike on the other side of the mountain?"

"No, I'm only saying that we shouldn't discount the fact that McLeod could have had a money maker. And what I am thinking is that this Town could use a good financial shot in the arse and... this could be it. That's all I'm saying!"

"So, I think that even if McLeod's mine is worthless, it is still the only respectful way to pay our last respects to him for his gift, is to make the effort to give him a proper burial." Said the Mayor.

"Respect!" Smooth snorted. Every day, fresh out of bed he got a spike of pain in his left knee where McLeod hit him with an axe handle on one of his drunken visits to Lone Bull before sobering up enough to offer a water weak apology before leaving Lone Bull with his supplies.

"You don't want to forget that the ground is still frozen five foot down and it won't be thawed until May when we can dig a proper grave!" Said Crank "And we can't do that with the front-blade without taking out half of the Tow! Also Right now, I got a contract to open the Pass with the backhoe and that is going to take a fair amount of time to do the job after the avalanche packed it rock hard".

The Mayor digested the reality of the situation and his mind raced ahead to the next obstacle. "So, what to do with the body until then?"

"Where's the body now?" Asked Mrs. Tashoots. .

"In the cold-room at the back of my store, but it can't stay there any longer. My cat 'Biscuit' got into it last night and chewed on one of McLeod's legs!" "

Brand blanched when he heard this and fought to clear the image from his mind of a cat eating on a human appendage in the General Store next to the bacon he may have had for breakfast.

"That's why I didn't ask our visiting priest Father Sullivan to be here. You know how the Church... and the Police, are about bodies in disrepair."

Exasperated, the older Fenton asked, "So what do you suggest?"

"It's already frozen." Said Brand. "And where are you going to find a round coffin?"

The room fell silent.

"Well, I've given it some thought," said Chance, "and I think I've come up with something. Why not thaw the body out, straighten it out, remove the chunk of spruce, and I'll order a cheap coffin from Whitehorse? When it gets here, we'll fill it with water, set it outside and refreeze it. Then bury him in the graveyard in the Spring when the ground is thawed!"

"We're going to have to do that anyway." Observed the older Mrs. Tashoots.

"Well, I might be able to get the Provincial Coroner's office to help with the coffin costs. Maybe they have some spare coffins laying around, or maybe they could help us financially It doesn't have to be fancy one.

Suddenly another idea ignited the Mayor. "What if we throw a big party at the Recreation Centre ... we'll call it a 'Wake' for McLeod!" He smiled.

"And at it we can announce the Will and part about issuing stock shares to everyone."

"Everyone?" Asked Smooth thinking about the Landers

representatives.

"Yeah!" Said Chance definitively, for he saw no separation in the three communities. "If we do the stock-share idea that our Mayor here has been going on about, we will all, everyone in the Valley including the Landers share equally in getting McLeod planted".

"And, if we do it that way everyone will come to the dance because there is a financial gain in it. Besides, it will be Spring soon, and a good time for a good blow-out!"

"Great idea!" Now exclaimed Smooth "We'll thaw the body out, straighten it out and lay it out in the coffin, nice and good and proper".

Feeling on a common track, the Mayor then laid out the complete idea. "We'll fill the coffin with water, freeze it solid, store it some place until Spring-thaw when we can get the backhoe to dig a plot in the graveyard."

"In a coffin, and the promise of financial gain, people will be more accepting of sharing the meat house. For the time, at least until the body can be thawed enough to straighten it out to get it into a coffin, I can keep it back in the empty storage building that I never use and it is unheated. But once we get it in a coffin it is the back of the meat house AND don't anyone broadcast the fact that it is there. Some people won't like it that their Winter's meat is stored with a human body."

The Mayor looked around the room. "So, then it is settled, we'll straighten him out put him in the coffin, hold a "Wake" for him announce the terms of the Will! and Bob's your Uncle!"

Chance nodded, "I'll get a coffin, and when the casket gets here, we'll put McLeod in it, fill it with water and let it freeze solid, and then quietly keep it in the meat house until Spring, dig a grave in the graveyard, and without another 'never-you-mind', we're owners in his mine!" He smiled, "AGREED?!" Everyone nodded

The idea caught everyone's imagination. Especially the part about a "Wake" and was unanimously adopted.

"Hey!! I have another idea, that part about the "Wake". We could hold it at the Recreation Building. Invite everyone in the Valley. Do everybody good to have an after the Winter blowout." said Smooth. "And about the part the cat chewed upon McLean's leg, he's going to hell anyway, chewed or unthawed!" Snapped the Mayor. "That's disrespectful and I don't appreciate that kind of talk in the Council Chambers!"

"Well, get used to it because I think having that bastard in the Winter Meat Locker of the store is going to be a load of hurt.

"I have another idea." Said Smooth not taking any of the dialogue seriously. "Get the coffin. Fill it with the body, fill it, freeze it solid. and we clandestinely stash it out on the lake with a rope to tow it back to land when the ground has thawed I say either drag it out onto the lake for the wolves or wait until forest fire season and do a cremation".

"Stop!" Barked Mrs. Tashoots, "This is why we call you our 'Younger Brothers'. Why not just fly it over to Whitehorse with Chris, until the summer then give him a proper burial? It is because you think like children!" She paused.

"Has anyone heard from Chris?" The room fell silent!

After considerable debate it was settled for the Council to go with the plan of freezing the flooded coffin, keeping it in the back of the community meat house with a tag and leaving it at that! No one was happy about the morgue, and the Village suddenly experienced a record of vegetarian converts.

Out of "Meeting Fatigue", everyone agreed.

Chapter 9

The Vancouver Club is an elegant historical institution nestled like a mushroom in a forest of sequoia trees. Once this brick and stone four story mansion had a commanding view of Vancouver, the Fraser Harbour and the North Shore mountains beyond, but today it is all but hidden by skyscrapers most towering many stories above the Club's roofline. The Vancouver Club is "Private", membership by invitation only, and for decades it was "Male Only" but that changed as women became executives! Still, even as membership changed, historical tradition hangs on the walls with the seventy-year-old tapestries and sixty-year-old butlers who have served the patrons for fifty of them.

Ironically, though surrounded by the towering glass buildings, the Vancouver Club is where monumental deals are concocted and concluded for grandiose projects like giant hydro-electrical dams, miles of free-ways and multi-billion-dollar gold mines mostly over lunch meetings.

Marvin Evans got to the Club first before his guest. He gave his key to his private liquor lock box in a wall of cubicles resembling a rural post office. The difference between the two was that instead of packages and letters, the contents of these boxes were exotic and expensive liquor bottles as with a rural post office, they were privately personal, the difference was these were not for mail. but rather the key holder's preferred booze.

"Will you be lunching alone?" Asked the tuxedoed waiter retrieving Marvin's bottle of Jack Daniels 'Special Blend' from the wall of his private box. He set it on the table, accompanied by a pitcher of water and glass tumbler full of ice cubes.

"No." He smiled taking the bottle of whiskey and the glass from the waiter. "His name is Mister Wattley. When he arrives, please put our tab on my account. He will not be a member; he is my personal guest. I left his name with the doorman."

"Very good Sir."

Soon a tall, well-tanned man in a beige blazer was escorted to Marvin's table.

"Michael! Good of you to come. Any trouble parking?"

"I took a cab," smiled the man. "I didn't want to deal with down-town traffic this time of day."

No sooner had he sat down then immediately the waiter came to the table with a variety of ties folded across his arm.

"I'm sorry, I forgot to tell you that ties are mandatory in the Club's Main Dining Room." He said to his guest

The visitor looked at the selection of ties and chose one.

"What do you think?"

"Excellent selection, goes with your shirt."

"Would the gentleman like a drink from the bar?" The waiter asked.

"I'll have what he's having."

"Very good Sir."

Soon the waiter returned with a glass tumbler with ice.

"So, what's up?" Marvin's guest asked.

"Well, maybe nothing, but here is the story. In the north-west Yukon on the East end of Kolsana Lake, there is a small town called Lone Bull".

"Yes, I remember the name from years back when a Mining conglomerate had a very profitable gold mine there." He paused for a moment. "Didn't the ore body suddenly vanish without a trace?"

"That's right, but there was a town that survived out of the mining operation, and somehow it still exists, mainly retired miners and a few government support people, like a nurse and teachers. Currently the Yukon Hydroelectric people are there surveying to elevate the Lake for a huge dam to feed the Territory's electrical system".

Michael smiled, "Yea, I remember the place. I was there fishing about a decade ago. In fact, when the mine was running it was a very productive one, as I remember, and they were getting exceptional gold concentrate out of it. But then, like you say, " he paused for a moment, "it vanished!"

"That's right, the parent company poured a lot of money into it trying to find where the vein went, but they couldn't find it.. and as you know, eventually, except for a few retired miners, some maintenance people, and a few stores for necessities like groceries, a hardware store etc, plus a Native Village and a school down on the Lake; when the mining company pulled out stock and barrel, the town shrunk significantly... but, amazingly, it didn't die.!"

"That's right, and that was the situation up until recently. However, there was this one miner, actually a 'powder monkey' who ...."

Michael looked quizzically at him. "A what?"

"You know the guys that loads and explodes the drill holes with dynamite." He waited a moment until his guest nodded.

"Anyway this 'powder-monkey', had a novel idea about what had happened to the orebody, specifically, that half of the mountain collapsed under the weight of a massive ice field above and...!" Marvin paused for drama.

"So, the miner went around to the back of the mountain and plotted the direction from the mine side of the mountain where the vein might go, and he started tunnelling from the opposite side of the mountain looking for it."

"Also, though the fact that there was once a very profitable gold mine on Lone Bull Peak, no one reached the same conclusion as the miner. His name was Mcleod." Michael nodded.

"So now race ahead. A few weeks into this Spring, the mountains surrounding Bennet Lake, the one above Lone Bull... and of course the road over the one pass out to Whitehorse was closed by a massive set of avalanches."

The maître de' nodded to Marvin that his dining table was ready.

After studying the menu and ordering, Evan's guest looked at Marvin. "And?!" He asked,

"Right! So here is the deal... and ... at first, you'll think it is a concoction of "Bull Shit", but it's the truth. The Miner, his last name was, as I said, McLeod, left a Will stating that when he died he was leaving title to his claim and surrounding properties to the people of Lone Bull and the corresponding Indian village down on the Lake... with the stipulation that when he died, he be given a regular burial, with a proper headstone in the Town's cemetery in exchange for the rights to the property he owned.

"So, you think there may something to it!"

"All I know is when I talked with a lawyer named Brand in Lone Bull who had drafted McLeod's will, he said that he was paid for his services in gold!"

"So you think...?"

"I don't know ... but just in case, it might be worth-while to get a couple of young geologists to go up there and poke around. The lawyer said they were forming a public company, and all of the legal residents of the Valley would be issued shares. So... if the mine does look promising, we might be able to get it by just buying out the shareholders." He smiled, enjoying watching his friend's face.

"And, as I understand it, they are not only going to form a company of all of eligible people in the Valley as the shareholders, they are talking about listing it on the Vancouver Stock Exchange. And get this, the name of the company is the "Lone Bull Bonanza"!

Their waiter returned to say their table for lunch was ready. It was a great table with a commanding view of the Harbour, the Stanley Park Bridge and the Coastal range to the North.

"I don't even know if what they are doing is legal, but it may be worth-while, like I said to send a couple of geologists up there to poke around."

"Great idea, but we don't want to tip our hand." He thought for a moment "There is one established mine exploration company that I work with, who could send a couple of geologists into the area to investigate without triggering any bells. But...!" Marvin looked hard at his friend, "They can't mention what we are up to."

"If the property defined by the miner's Will does have something, we want to secure ownership before anyone else can."

"I'll get right on it this afternoon."

Chapter 10

For five more days Maktu was kept in a state of induced unconsciousness as the doctors scrambled to stabilise his overall vital signs. He was recovering remarkably well but there were complications. The tissue around his eyes where his goggles had been before being ripped off during the accident, was severely frost bitten and required some skin grafts.

The nurse in Lone Bull had done a marvellous job of treating him for acute hypothermia. It was largely because his heavy clothing but also the body-bag had slowed the heat-loss and so had his skin responded well... all except for his left hand! He had arrived at her door without a mitten, likely removed before the man had gone into the water.

Also, the Whitehorse optometrist had treated numerous cases of snow-blindness and had developed a special lens that corrected for both situations of too much light and not enough light in the dark. The frame design was like a mountaineer's goggles or an incognito rock star. Finally, using only pain killers Maktu was allowed a window of consciousness, and the doctor decided it was time to allow Maktu some reprieve from his induced coma.

"Do you know where you are?" he asked Maktu when he was brought into the well-lit hospital surgery, Maktu squinted as his eyes scanned the well-lit room.

"Hollywood?"

"Close." The Doctor nodded his head, "very close... Whitehorse, Yukon".

The doctor smiled and proceeded to tell Maktu the events around the accident and the current situation. Most notably that there was an important decision the doctor had to make... mainly that Maktu's left hand was severely frost-bitten when Maktu took off his mitten to grasp the knife to cut Shag free of his harness that tied him to the sled submerging with snow-machine. As a consequence, on his left hand his little finger and ring finger had been already removed due gangrene from lack of circulation and tissue freezing.

It was the remaining fingers on his left hand that concerned the doctor. And he needed the patient to help with the decision to try to save at least the thumb and two fingers. It was a critical decision he didn't want to make alone, and he explained the situation to the man.

The Doctor paused for a moment. "I need you to help me make a decision about your left hand!"

"First, are you right or left-handed?

"Left." Maktu said. "I do everything with my left hand... write, shoot a gun, but mainly I paint with my left hand.

"What do you for a living?" The doctor asked, though he knew the answer, he had seen some of Maktu's work scattered around Whitehorse; the Yukon Hotel, the Airport and a few homes of various friends... they were all exceptional. "Damn!" The Doctor swore under his breath.

He looked long at Maktu. He took out a pen. "Here. Take this.'" And he held up a fountain pen in front of Maktu, hoping he would not fumble and drop it.

By instinct, Maktu reached with his left hand, and in spite of the bandages and the tender stumps where two fingers had been., he took hold of the pen with a firm, controlled grasp.

"Get used to it!" The Doctor smiled.

"I'm going to hold you for a couple more days, and if you're careful to take care of your damaged left hand, I'll discharge you."

"As I gather, if it weren't for your dog and a guardian angel at the Nurse's Station there in Lone Bull, you'd be in a body-bag in the morgue!"

After letting the words settle, the doctor spoke again. "Unfortunately, you'll have to stay with us for a few more days but hopefully we can salvage your three remaining fingers. And hopefully you can paint again."

Chapter 11

"Marlo, would you come in?" Brandon spoke to the slightly ajar wooden door to the Gallery's inner office where the masterpieces rested beneath staggering prices. "When is Maktu's show scheduled to arrive?"

A tall slender woman in a sleek dress of expensive material that bent the light to her statuesque frame, did not look up as she entered, her eyes scanning the double binder schedule book. She ran the gallery from the schedule book. Everything from bookings, media coverage, hotel rooms for the artists, art prices, art placement within the gallery.

Brandon, the owner of the Sullivan Gallery, had the instincts that come from three generations of successful art dealers mainly because they loved what they did, and they were an artist's dealer. Their talent was taking the exceptional and giving them a platform with first, loyalty to the artists. Some artists never caught with the public, but those who did, such as Picasso, Riopelle and Jackson Pollock were loyal.

Much to his embarrassment, Brandon was doomed to the stature of a big man, who carried himself slightly stooped so as not to tower over other people. His hands were catcher mitts, yet he had the long fingers of a classical pianist. His face was long and rectangular with curious eyes and an accepting smile.

He made the decisions, planned the shows but his main focus was on the artists he booked. As a consequence, he easily secured important showings, as did his father and grandfather, focusing on the Masters of the time. Marlo's job was to make it happen.

His grandfather had, at the age of fifteen swum the Olga River in nineteen nineteen. He worked construction, and where others sought the easy jobs of robots, he sought those of risk for they paid the most. Where others put their money into personal things, he bought land, farmland on an Island called Manhattan Island. In fact, he bought the property on which the Gallery now sat.

"Here, read this." Brandon pushed a print-out of an email he'd just received from Maktu via a nurse at the Whitehorse Hospital. Marlo didn't like the implication, and an anxious feeling seized her.

Dear Mr. Sullivan

"This is being dictated to you by a nurse for reasons soon to be obvious. There has been a change of plans. I've had an accident coming out from my cabin … luckily it happened at a lake landing near the town of Lone Bull, and thanks to my dog and a smart nurse, I am alive... but I am having to dictate this from the Whitehorse hospital!

I'm told the air was minus 50 degrees! All I recall is the snow-machine was sinking fast, pulling the sled with it. I vaguely recall taking off my glove grabbing my scabbard knife and cutting free Shag's harness and the cargo straps before the machine pulled the cargo sled under."

"Oh my God!" Marlo gasped, looking up at Brandon, who was watching intently her reaction. The writing stopped at the bottom of the first page and her hands raced to the next page.

"I vaguely recall," the letter began again, *"my clothes filling with ice-water, making movement like swimming near impossible and I was being pulled down … though fighting against it".*

"Here's the part you're not going to believe." said Brandon.

" Suddenly, as my head was being pulled under for the last time, I felt something lifting me back to the surface. I believe it was the pack of paintings that was so over-packed in water-tight layers that it heaved to the surface underneath my dog and me and essentially saved our lives when I had given up hope!"

"The rest of the story is how Shag dragged me to shore and finally to a nearby cabin that belonged to the Village nurse, Anyway, I was medic-vaced out to Whitehorse where I was rushed into intensive care and have been the project of a team of doctors who specialise in severe frostbite".

"The upshot is, the paintings that were supposed to be in Manhattan are gone! They were in the bundle that carried me to the surface, but they were strapped to the back sled and snowmobile that sunk as far as I know, to the bottom of the lake"

"All of the skin around my eyes where the fur on the hood of my parka didn't cover is blistered and has turned black and I have had skin grafts and I have to wear mountaineer glasses to protect the skin and still let me see. Unfortunately, all the tissue that was exposed directly to the water and cold, including my left hand are in pretty bad shape. Especially, the hand I'd pulled off my glove from to use my knife for cutting my dog Shag free of his tether".

The hard news is, two fingers on my left hand (I'm left-handed) became gangrenous and had to be cut off! Unfortunately, the bundle of paintings that essentially saved my life has disappeared, presumably to the bottom into the lake.'

"Again, I'm sorry to let you down."

Maktu

She liked Maktu though she'd never met him. In her mind, he was this kind of rugged but incredibly gifted version, as she coined, of a grizzly-dundee. She'd known in the city many men who were 'wanna-be wilderness men', boasting about going deep into the frozen north, living off the land. Fantasizing a full day snowmobile ride out from his winter cabin to civilisation. She had been stunned when she saw the paintings Brandon had brought back with him from his latest fishing trip up North. Spectacular scenery, beautifully haunting. An impressionist style wholly his own.

Chapter 12

“John,” Chance radio-phoned the Director and Owner of the ‘Whitehorse Funeral Home’. “I need to ask if you have a cheap coffin for a regular sized male, roughly 150 pounds and 5 foot, 6 inches tall. Nothing fancy, in fact very ordinary! The main criteria is cheap!” He went on to explain the situation with the emphasis again upon “cheap!”

“Your lucky day my friend. An older woman here in Whitehorse purchased one a couple of months ago, even paid in advance for the coffin and embalming.” The Mortician said. “But she died in a house fire that totally consumed her residence AND her body to ashes!”

“So, I can give you a deal on the coffin. Discounting the embalming of course.”

“Actually, It was the man’s wishes that he NOT be embalmed but actually frozen in a coffin and buried as is”.

“It is a little unorthodox and I don’t know what the Mounties might say about it, but from my standpoint the coffin is yours! However, you have to pay for the shipping,” Then the Mortician added. “And I don’t want to know anything about how or what you do with it. As far as I’m concerned, you just bought a box the equivalent of a case of Campbell’s soup”.

“Great!” said Chance.

"You will have to get a Mountie or some medical authority to sign-off on the cause of death. How did he die?"

"Hypothermic shock"

"You got anyone there who can sign off on Natural Causes?"

Chance thought a moment. "Actually, we do! She is a certified nurse and has a ticket as an Emergency Mortician's Assistant".

"That should be enough as long as there is no sign of 'foul play'."

"I don't think there is, we got the body yesterday and he hasn't moved from where we left him overnight".

"You sure he's dead?"

"Dead as a snowball in the Arctic! But send the casket ASAP and pray for an Arctic front to keep it that way!"

"How about shares in a gold mine?"

Chapter 13

Maktu edged to a corner near the door where two groups of young Tahltan teenagers gathered on the perimeter of the adults. Shy boys pumped with co-brother courage asked giggling girls in jean jackets to dance. And even though they might be petting in the church basement at night, no hands touched on the way to the dance floor. And, if the song was fast, there was no contact at all. If too much interest was shown in front of the elders, the couple of focus would be a subject mirroring the current status of family feuds or approvals, and either way, they became an item, subjected to dour looks or approving looks for the rest of the evening

Maktu watched with amusement their carefully controlled behaviour. Then suddenly he saw a non-Native woman standing between both the gathering of the K'sewet people and the Anglo residents from Lone Bull. She was the Valley's public nurse and what he'd learned from the doctor in Whitehorse, her quick thinking had saved his life. And he wanted to approach her and thank her for essentially saving his life, but his bush nurtured shyness held him back

Adding to his discomfort standing beside her was the Provincial Hydro geologist stationed there to keep the hydro-electro station operating. But when the woman saw Maktu their eyes locked.

Christ! He felt like one of the fool teenagers. He studied her face. It was a tomboy face complete with freckles. Her body was like a lanky young colt. He saw her mouth move, then realised she was talking to someone next to her. It was Richard Bonner; the Yukon Hydro technician located in Lone Bull to keep the power station operating.

Bonner caught Maktu's eyes and turned to Christina wondering who he was.

Christina looked directly at him. He knew her from afar in that she was the Valley's nurse, and he reasoned, likely the person who had treated him for hypothermia and made arrangements for him to be medic-vaced and her face lit-up, she turned to Bonner and suddenly the two started coming across the dance floor towards him. He wanted to bolt but he remained still, if for no other reason than gratitude.

"So, how are you?" She asked absently reaching for Maktu's hand and then stopping abruptly when she saw the bandages.

"I spoke with Dr. Moresby. He was concerned about the gangrene, and he said that for a while he was not sure you would live."

"He told me" Maktu said to Christina, "that you saved my life!" He smiled at her. "Thanks!"

"I don't know about that, but your dog definitely did save your life. As far as I can tell he dragged you soaking wet from where you crashed into the ice jam to my doorstep!" Then she suddenly laughed. "And he was definitely persistent, barking and howling above the storm until I opened up".

"He always had an eye for pretty women" Maktu laughed. "Where is he?"

"At my cabin...:" She paused for a moment smiling. "Living the life of luxury with all of the food the neighbours have been dropping off. Loin cuts of caribou, moose." She laughed. "He even had grizzly liver that the Tollans, next door had been saving for a special occasion." She laughed, Maktu laughed for he guessed that the smell of cooked bear liver would be pretty revolting for someone not raised on it.

"By the way, what's his name?"

"Shag."

"Shag? Oh my God! A beautiful animal like that and his name is 'Shag'.. like a carpet?" Christina snapped astonished.

"Exactly. But the truth is when he was a puppy he was always 'shagging' along with me, my constant companion, we grew up together. When can I come get him?"

"Anytime." Christina spoke with a smile and an inclination to her voice that meant exactly that!

"Welcome home." Said the Hydro engineer who monitored the dam. "Any sign of Chris?"

Maktu knew him only by sight in town and one meeting on the lake when he was doing a survey for the electrical company that controlled the height of the lake via an electrical dam. Presently it was a small, low head dam producing enough energy for both K'weset and Lone Bull. But it was built in a critical place that one day, with a few million tonnes of concrete and steel the lake could be a major electrical supplier for western Canada given enough head.

"I gather there has been no news about Chris. I flew with him a few times. He was an excellent pilot".

"We know each other." said Maktu watching Richard's reaction closely to see if he remembered. He saw him flinch. At the right time he would remind the Hydro man of times when he was down river making the lake higher, testing for projected effects of flood that he never saw the 'Splendour'. But he turned his attention to Christine. She blushed but it bloomed into a smile. He smiled back.

"I swam in her eyes," was a phrase Maktu's Grandfather said when he spoke of first meeting Maktu's Grandmother. Maktu swam in Christina's eyes. She smiled back.

"I'm very sorry about Chris. I flew with him once, you know." He said to Christina trying to interrupt the energy between them both.

"You, and nine tenths of the people in the North."

"I thought he was an excellent pilot." Richard continued.

Maktu thought for a moment considering the comment. "He couldn't have been too good..." Maktu leaned close to the electrical engineer. "He's dead!"

"You shouldn't see it that way. You don't know for sure; he could walk in here any day; stranger things have happened." The Hydro lineman tried to break the tension.

"Fuck man! He's dead!" Maktu suddenly barked, "and there's no fucking reason to pretend!" He glared at the Hydro man, all of the frustration of having to finally accept the reality of the man's statement came to a boil.

Realising the issue was near a flash point, Christina grabbed Maktu's hand and jerked him onto the dance floor. "Come!" She barked!

Maktu didn't dance. He'd never danced. He felt rude and awkward. But Christina didn't care, she moved with enough freedom to carry both of them comfortably. With her smile she held his attention, her eyes locked on his; and she placed her hands to his back, drawing his hips to hers. Leading him lightly around the floor, he felt insular to everyone, their's was something beyond the two of them.

"Have you ever danced blind?" She asked.

"Sober?" He smiled, thought then for a minute. "Is it like anatomy lessons by brail?"

"Exactly!" She grinned and gave him a gentle tug. "Try it. Close your eyes and give me your good hand, I'll lead." Maktu was surprisingly willing to follow. At first, they slowly circled clockwise. He felt her curl into his arms. and for a moment she pressed her body against him, before suddenly rolling away with a snap to the music.

Then immediately he was drawn by her to follow her lead. He felt her arm wrap around him. He was startled and tried to pull back, but her grip held him close.

He gave a light tug to test the sincerity of her restraint not to separate. She held on with equal strength which he wasn't prepared for, and he opened his eyes and became lost in hers. She was smiling, intentionally holding him. Maktu looked quickly about to confirm that no one was watching, then suddenly with enough punch to the music to justify their intimacy, she pushed him back and then snapped him back into her. "Dance as though you're blind." She whispered.

Maktu broke free, trying to get some distance before the two were caught but too late. He opened his eyes and everyone in the immediate vicinity were looking at them. He grinned sheepishly which only served to make Christina laugh even harder. But still, only when the song ended did Maktu open his eyes fully and for a moment they hugged, then followed the crowd towards the exit sweating with the sweat of a turned-up sauna. Many headed outside to cool off, great streams of steam rose up into the sub-zero air.

"Now aren't you ashamed of yourself for never dancing blind." Her hair wet from the dance, melted the snowflakes leaving little droplets. She leaned her head forward shaking her long auburn hair around her face, letting the night air cool the back of her neck. Maktu was reminded of a young horse shaking out its mane after a hard run. She pitched her head backwards and brushed it loosely into place with her fingers. The light from the hall caught the droplets...

"So that's how the blind dance?" He said in awe of the moment.

He liked being with her.

"Tell you the truth, I've never seen a blind person dance."

"That makes you equal with them, I doubt they have ever seen you dance!"

It was the beginnings of a relationship so strong that words were seldom necessary, and even then, the expression fell far short of the moment.

The Dance was well on its way when the Valley Fiddlers saw the Mayor's intentions and set up a medley of three fast songs in a row. The only way to calm down the crowd was dance them through the floorboards. And when they finished the set both dancers and musicians were sweating and gasping for air.

"If I may have your attention." Said the Mayor of Lone Bull. No one responded. "You're attention please!" Still nothing. Convinced that the mike was dead he unknowingly carried it close to an amplifier and an ear- splitting squawk silenced the Hall.

"Sorry. I didn't know that would happen", he apologised after a fiddler had to run across the stage and remove the mike from the Mayor's hands. Mayor Jarvis took centre stage. There were so few occasions in Lone Bull for the Mayor to command an audience, he was anxious to make the most of this opportunity. He hoped no one would notice that his pants didn't quite match the jacket and vest. The trousers that went with the suit had a hole the shape of his iron, so did his ironing board. It hadn't been a good day.

In his haste to thaw Mcleod out of his foetal position, when the body moved in, his wife moved out – he accidentally roasted part of the miner's shoulder by having him too close to the stove, and the stove too hot for mere thawing. It was the smell that made him aware something was wrong, just like it was the smell of the burning trousers that awakened him to the calamity of roasting flesh. Thirty below and the doors wide open! but still it stunk! God, he hoped no one would notice, 'I'll never get re-elected', he worried.

"Any reason to bring out the Valley is a joyous Occasion!" He started his well-practised speech. "But let us not forget that this is also a solemn occasion."

There was still too much joy for the Mayor's likening. "I said a 'solemn' event!" Frustrated, he motioned for the pallbearers to bring in the casket. Two sawhorses were placed at the foot of the stage, directly below the speaker.

"What's that smell?" Asked one of the pall- bearers. Standing on the stage he still thought he caught the odd whiff of charred meat. Hopefully they would think it was one of the bush hippie's supper-dishes in the kitchen.

"We are gathered here to pay our last respects to one of our own." The Mayor said into the microphone. "He was a man of different ways... but a man anyway!" He liked that phrase. "Sure, there were times when we had differences with McLeod. There was a spell when he was 'mental' but being bushed ain't new to any of us".

"I ask you. How many could live the way he did and keep our nuggets bundled. Not many, I suspect."

"But Mcleod was more than a man, he was a symbol of the human spirit at the edge of the wilderness. He had the same perseverance that brought the first foreign hunters and trappers, and then miners to our Valley."

"And, without, the sacrifice of men and women like McLeod, would any of us be here now!' Various Natives looked at each other wondering what their contribution to the humans already in habitation of the, as the Mayor called it, "wilderness".

"Think about that. We are the leading edge of civilisation, but we are nothing without a few humans like McLeod at the cutting edge of the face of the axe of mankind!"

It made no difference to the Mayor that his metaphor was thin as morning ice, and significantly blind to the Native people who had lived on the land way before the European newcomers. No, the phrase occurred to him while doing dishes and that was enough for inclusion.

"So, in accordance with the Lone Bull's Town Council decision and presumably the departed's wishes, there will now be a reading of McLeod's will. And I'm told it affects everyone, so listen up!" Then an after-thought occurred to him. "Also, the ladies auxiliary has prepared a supper for us afterwards!" He stopped speaking and surveyed the crowd

"So, at this time I'd like the Town Lawyer, Gordon Brand to read the Will."

Brand took the microphone. "I James Arnold Mcleod being of sound mind and body do here-by make the following bequest. To the residents of the K'weset and Lone Bull, and the 'Down Landers'. I leave my mine, the "Big Bonanza." ... on the provision that I'm given a proper burial in the Lone Bull cemetery. And it is my wish for a proper hardwood casket and a grave six feet deep with a proper headstone." It was signed by the miner and witnessed "Gordon Brand".

There was some discussion about what the bequest meant. Most people figured the mine was a madman's obsession, fighting his demons against the face of a granite mountain. Still, anything free was worth some attention. On the other hand, funerals in the winter were a known impossibility so the likelihood of fulfilling the miner's wishes seemed remote.

"Just how do you plan on planting him?" Someone asked.

"Freeze him!" Said the Mayor, proud of the Council's obvious decision. Tonight, after the Wake, we'll fill the casket with water and let it freeze solid. Then we can put it in the back of the meat-house until Spring when we can get a backhoe to bury him." It sounded reasonable.

"So, what if you do get him buried, how we supposed to share a mine, supposing its worth more than a popcorn fart, which I strongly doubt?!"

"No need to talk like that Barney." The Mayor spoke up. "I'm feeling really positive about all this. This mine could be the thing that turns the Valley around. Who knows, he might have hit the missing vein from the Lone Bull Mine."

"Maybe you think I'm a fool, but I'm certain we'll look back on this night as the beginning of a new morn." (How 'Night' could be 'Morn' didn't throw the Mayor). He smiled his best campaign grin, "You all know what I always say, I'm bullish on Lone Bull!" He basked in the creativeness of his well-worn statement.

"But to answer your question, the regional board has had a meeting, and we've struck upon a plan that would allow everyone to share equally."

"Our idea is to form a 'Company' and issue shares equally to all legal residents of the Watershed that have been here more than a year... of course, this is all subject to your approval."

"How many shares you plan on issuing?"

"We'd have to see what is there — what the mine potential is by doing some "drift drilling." The Mayor flaunted his newly acquired knowledge of mining. "If the tests show high-grade, we could be talking Big Money! Maybe an outside company like Amax or Noranda would want in., and we'd have to have stock split. On the other hand, if the hole proves poor, what's lost by issuing a lot. To answer your question.... a quarter of a million shares! For starters!"

Whether the shares were worth two cents or two thousand dollars per person, it made no difference, two thousand of anything was impressive and there was suddenly a general sense of wealth in the room. Louie-Louie from K'weset calculated it out to a thousand shares per person.

There were a few 'nay-sayers', as the Mayor called anyone who argued that nothing of nothing was still nothing, but the growing feeling in the room was that maybe... McLeod maybe wasn't such a bad guy after-all!

The line to the kitchen passed by the coffin and after the reading of the Will the body got a lot more reverence... one woman even whispered, "Thank you!"

Finally, after the dance and the communal supper, Maktu walked Christina down the hill to her cabin in the Village of K'weset before catching a ride back to the airbase and the last search and rescue flight in the morning. Christina found Maktu easy to talk with and told him about her life on the East Coast of the United States in the State of Pennsylvania.

"Come to supper tomorrow, I have something special for you".

"My dog?" He smiled.

"More important!!" She smiled.

"Come back tomorrow night after you finish with the Search and Rescue flight "Yep, something more valuable than your hound!" Christina smiled.

"Sorry to disappoint you, but nothing is more important than Shag." He added, but his curiosity was sparked.

"Come tomorrow for supper and you'll see." She smiled.

Chapter 14

The final flight of the giant Hercules "Search and Rescue" plane produced still no more results and that evening the official Search was called off, though the file would still be open with an "Unresolved" stamp on the "Flight Mission" folder in the Whitehorse Aeronautics section of the Territorial Government Offices.

Deeply disappointed, his heart aching, he was still resolved to enjoy the supper with Christina and, of course, to retrieve Shag. Though he remembered nothing of the Lake crash, he was told in detail by his doctor how Shag had saved his life.

Christina was sitting on the front porch of the Nurse's Station cabin, Shag laying beside her feet. When he saw Maktu he leapt to his feet and lunged off the porch as though a grizzly bear had just arrived.

"Shag!" Maktu called out and immediately the dog's tail began to wag. He hit Maktu so hard that the Indian staggered losing his balance.

"Did you think you'd never see me again!" Maktu grabbed the big dog by the jowls which made the dog jump up and down against Maktu then he broke away and started to run in circles around him.

"OK... OK. That's enough you're going to hurt someone!"

Maktu laughed and grabbed the dog and shook his head. "Come, sit before you hurt someone and I have to leave you here again!" Christina laughed. Maktu sat down beside her as they watched the dog tear around out of joy after presumably thinking he'd never see Maktu again.

They sat on the steps to her cabin talking about events in the Village and drinking tea, the final rays of the sun etched cloud shadows on the faces of the setting sun. "Oh!"Christina gasped and leapt to her feet causing Shag who lay between them on the front porch, to startle to his feet.

"After dinner, I have something for you more valuable than your hound!" Christine smiled.

"Sorry to disappoint you," he rose smiling, "but nothing is more important than Shag." He added, but his curiosity was sparked.

The dog simply lifted an eyebrow, looked at Maktu, turned to Christina and his tail gave another tail wag which surprised Maktu. Shag had had but one owner, but obviously he had expanded his sights.

"T.L.C ... Tender Loving Care". She grinned. "Of course, it doesn't hurt that he has become the Village mascot, and has had a steady diet of caribou, moose, deer, and occasionally a store-bought dog-biscuit! "

"Oh Good." Maktu sighed and scuffed his dog's neck.

"And you?" He looked at her. Her smile was even more captivating than it was in the moonlight when they first met at the dance.

"Well, to tell you the truth, I'm a little sad that you are taking my friend." She too started petting the dog.

"He's been such good company. And... very popular in the Village. In fact, every morning on my front porch there's something new for him, and not the odd dog-biscuits but huge chunks of meat and like I said, a variety ... moose, caribou, elk, deer. Now he won't touch the canned food I bought at the store."

She stopped petting Shag and smiled at Maktu. "Won't you come in? I've taken the liberty of fixing us some supper, not as good as Shag has grown used to, I'm afraid."

The smells were delightful particularly the intoxication of home-made bread. On the stove was a casserole he guessed was not Canadian.

"Ukrainian, that's my heritage. It's not much, but better than you get at Maude's Kitchen in Town."

'Maude's' was the requisite diner for times when the one other restaurant 'Sarah's Kitchen' was closed. Her cooking wasn't particularly special, but Maude's laugh was bountiful as was her waistline and her serving's matching her size.

Maktu was in awe at the complexity of smells. He hadn't had a home cooked meal in years. In fact, he had forgotten that people actually made an art out of cooking. Christina was obviously one of them who retained the skill and her heritage for exotic dishes.

"I hope you like Ukrainian cooking." She asked, studying his face.

"Ukrainian? I thought you said your last name is Williams?"

"I guess it depends on which Continent you're on."

She was easy to talk with. A happy person, the consequence, as he learned of a happy, healthy family raised in the posh suburbs of New York and attending a well-crafted and endowed girls school's school in Pennsylvania.

"Where did you learn to cook Russian dishes?"

"Ukrainian dishes," she bristled. "Both my Father and Mother are second generation from the Ukraine. Ukrainian is my second language, and when I go back for family reunions it is my first."

"I thought your last name was Williams?"

"As I said, it depends which continent you're on. Depends on if you are holding my passport, or... my birth certificate. You see my father's name was 'Prajasnuk' – pronounced 'Pra-hars-nuck'!"

She smiled, "Imagine going to a family reunion thinking your name is boringly Canadian, only to discover that the family's last name has more syllables than my entire English name." Her laugh was rich and full.

"And yours?" she asked.

He smiled. "Little Fox"

"Really!" She exclaimed, spooning the main course into a large serving-bowl, then stopping anticipating that he was kidding her.

"Really? Come on, I told you mine, fess-up."

"Well, ... translated into English it is 'Little Fox, but in Tlingit it is 'Da-de-ta-wana' and my dearest friend is named "Da-de-ba-bou"

"So, you are a real Indian?"

"And you're a real Ukrainian?"

Supper was incidental as they traded stories of their lives, each in a totally different wilderness – one truly wild, with the absence of man, one so crowded, that it too was a wilderness.

In the summer, Christina spent her time on her Grandparents' farm in Saskatchewan heaving hay bales, being, kicked by cows and learning to drive a tractor instead of a car.

Finally following the last course of fresh spring blueberry pie. Christina could hold back no longer and leapt to her feet. "Do you remember me telling you I was not just a pretty face and a keeper of your hound?

"No, I don't remember that at all!" Maktu laughed.

"Well, in fact I invited you here because of a surprise I have for you".

"Oh!" she said as a precursor thought before continuing. ".. would you mind closing that window against the wall across from the bed?" She pointed to an open window.

Maktu rose and went around the end of the bed, but there was a stack of something buried under a tarp between the bed and the window. "You'll have to move that junk first." She said.

Maktu nodded, watching her watching him as he walked around to the foot of her bed. On the floor there was a blanket-covered pile of something between him and the window.

"What are you going to do with that?" She asked. "It is your stuff?" She asked, a big grin on her face.

"That's where Shag prefers to sleep."

Maktu didn't understand. Christina came around the bed, by the window she bowed theatrically as a Ring Master of a Three-ring Circus might do. Dramatically she bent over, took two handfuls of the cover blanket and jerked it away.

"OH My GOD!" Maktu shrieked for there, just as he had bundled it weeks earlier, there was the bundle of his paintings!

"TA - DA!" She grinned!

"Oh my God!" He exclaimed again and tore at the knots, then peeled back each layer of industrial plastic. The painted canvases were all there, totally intact, and unstained, and as dry as the morning he'd meticulously make up the pack of his winter's work!

"But..." He stammered, "How did they survive the crash?!"

"The same could be asked of you...!"

"Do you mind if I open it up to see how much damage has been done?" He looked at her.

"Of course! They're yours" Christina smiled. "And" she grinned, "I want to see why everyone raves about your paintings." She smiled.

Soaked, then dried hard in the cabin heat, the tie-ropes

holding the pack intact had to be cut. Then with a deep sigh of fearful anticipation of what he'd find, he started unfolding each layer of the tarp down to the bottom painting-canvas which he carefully lifted and turned to the day light.

The canvas was completely dry! It shimmered afresh in the twilight light. Quickly he went through each canvas. Each was bone dry thanks the spacers that had kept them separated from the painting above and the one below.

"Oh my!" Christina gasped as each painted canvas appeared. She took each of them and placed it around the room. "They're beautiful!" She'd exclaimed; there were tears in her eyes.

"Look at this one!" She would hold up one to the light. "Now I see why everyone says what they say about you"

"Which is?"

She looked straight at him. "That you are a great artist!"

Much to Maktu's relief, the very last painting was as dry as the first. Maktu sat down astonished looking at the room full of canvases.

"Wow!" He shook his head. "I never thought I'd see them again, and especially in perfect condition!" He had prepared himself for the worst-case scenario; that the bundle had gone to the bottom of the lake with the sled... never to be recovered, and if it was, the bundle would have probably leaked, and the ice water would make the oil paint separate from the canvases.

"How did you recover them?" He asked astonished.

"I had nothing to do with it. The morning after your collision with the shore -ice, some of my students were going to school and saw that the coupling attaching the sled to the snowmobile had broken but it was sticking up out of the ice. So, when they came and told me and I told one of the parents who owned the backhoe that was retrieving the snowmobile, they hooked on the sled and recovered it too. They unloaded your stuff in the school gym, but

I thought that since you would be coming for Shag, I'd have the bundle brought here."

He was not sure if he kissed her out of gratitude, general exuberance, or maybe just because he'd wanted to kiss her after their very first dance.

"OH MY GOD!" He suddenly broke their embrace. "Do you have a fax machine?"

"Of course, this is the Nursing Station. Why?"

"I'd like to send a fax to Mr. Sullivan at his New York gallery". He looked at his bandaged left hand. "Could you do the typing?"

To Mr. Brandon Sullivan,

Sullivan Galleries, New York City.

Dear Sir,

If it is not too late, for your consideration, my paintings have been retrieved from a frozen lake, and they are all in perfect condition! As is the artist!"

If you still have some interest in viewing them with the possibility of showing any of them in your gallery. I have taken the liberty of photographing them and am forwarding the photos with this correspondence.

Attached you will find pictures of each canvas in case you still have any interest in my work. Specifically, there are a total of 40 works: twelve (8"X12"), twenty (24"X18"), seven (36"X48") and one very large landscape (48" X 42"). Also, they are mix of horizontal and vertical. Most of them are landscapes. All of them are studies in northern light.

If any of my winter's labours should interest you, I can arrange transportation of them to you in New York. Currently we are sealed off from overland access, but the airstrip, primitive as it is, is still open.

Thank you for your consideration, You can confirm reception of this message to this machine. I await your reply!

Sincerely, Maktu

They looked at each other as if for the first time. He took her hand with the undamaged one as if they had been holding hands for a long, long time. Christina glanced over at the baklava dish on the table. "Dessert?" She asked?

"Maybe later." He smiled.

Maktu and Christina agreed that the photographing be done only in the rich early morning light and methodically Maktu and Christina carefully took pictures of the entire collection. At Christina's insistence, she did a portrait shoot of Maktu. But at his insistence, he wore a glove over his left hand and the mountaineer glasses to mask the skin grafts around his eyes.

"This may be a waste of time." Maktu thought, but Christina assured him it definitely was not and sent the email. After the email and attachments were sent, Maktu and Christina developed a pattern. Each evening, they would meet on the beach, and one of them would start a fire and cook a camp supper of Maktu's making in a dutch-oven and watch the setting sun. Like teenagers they would hold hands, cautiously kiss, until finally Christina insisted that rather than Maktu returning to the apartment he'd shared with Chris at the airstrip, the Indian should spend the night

"Can I bring my dog?"

"Your dog!" She smirked, "He's our dog and you are my man!"

And without a change in their habits; Maktu continued to prepare supper over the campfire in the dutch-oven, and as the sun continued to set into the far Western shore of the lake, they held hands in silence and became a couple. And when it was time to leave, they washed what was left by Shag on the plates, packed-up and retired to Christina's cabin.

Then, one evening, when Christina appeared on the beach, much to her surprise, Maktu was not there, even though Shag, now programmed to the routine, jumped up from where he lay on the shore and came galloping up to meet her. But Maktu was obviously not around.

"No fire! No exotic supper!" She smiled, scolding Shag. "You haven't even started the fire!"

"He isn't supposed to. " Came a voice from behind.."It is time for something new!"

"New?" She asked, knowing there was more to come.

"As in New .... York!" He waved an envelope in his left hand. "It's from the gallery in New York, a Mister Sullivan".

"Is it a response to our email!' She asked.

Maktu was silent, letting the excitement linger.

"Yes! And he wants to have a show of the entire collection!"

He paused letting the words settle in. "And he wants the artist in attendance!"

Christina leapt into his arms. "Oh my God!"

"Wait... I'm not finished... and with a companion! Expenses covered – flight tickets, room at the Park Lane – Wherever that is!"

"OH MY GOD!" Christina exclaimed. "New York! And... the Park Lane. To my thinking, It is the nicest hotel in Manhattan! Sits right across the street from Central Park!"

"Will you come?" Maktu asked, but in truth he was begging. "I've never been out of the Yukon other than fighting fires in British Columbia., and that was only in a bush-plane or a chopper!"

"So, you're asking me, because you need a guide?" She teased.

"That and because I want to share this fantastic adventure with you".

"It'll be that for sure!" She smiled. "That and because I love you".

They were words he'd never said, and he was startled how easily they came. Christina told her friends and fellow teachers at the Village school about Maktu's invitation to go to New York... with a companion. And even though Shag would not be going she was going with Maktu.

Chapter 15

The geese were “lining up”, as Maktu’s grandmother would say when things were going right. But there was one uncertainty. And that was how much would he be paid by the Gallery and how would it happen? A flat amount for the show or a commission on sales? And how much would be the commission? Likely it would be based on a percentage of the sales, but he didn’t have any idea how much of a percentage.

And that was the pivotal point. If any of the paintings sold and that was big “if”, how much would make it into his pocket? No, he’d worry about that should it happen and when it happened, but not for now. To address his questions Christina encouraged him to call the Gallery owner directly.

A new radiophone system had been installed with salvaged towers from the Lone Bull mine. Because the system is shared with everyone, it is the glue that makes a web in the wilderness to hold a community and its communications together. The only disadvantage is, it is public. If you choose to listen, it is a live soap opera in the middle of the wilderness

There are both advantages and disadvantages to the radiophone. It is a lifeline for emergencies, a broadcaster of joy like the sound of a first grand child’s words can be shared on a radiophone. But the most important role of the radiophone is a safety net.

Because of the immediacy of contact when events don't go as planned it is invaluable. Chris, Maktu's pilot friend, spent much of his flying time responding to radio-phone emergencies into often questionable landing sites, under questionable conditions. He had delivered three babies, two of them were named Christopher.

The radiophone is not only a safety net it is often the foundation of sanity... but also a real soap-opera when there is no television.

In fact, the only drawback is that it is 'public'. A radiophone is essential, in two situations, a call for help in an emergency, but also of equal importance, an ointment to the wounds of Bush Fever... winter madness. When the lack of sun and snowdrifts cover the roof turning the inside of a cabin dark, the mind can spark a lot of delusions. At least with a radiophone there is comfort that others are going crazy as well.

Ecstatic that the Gallery offered to show his work, Maktu needed to speak on Christina's radiophone in her cabin, directly to Brandon Sullivan, the owner and curator of the Sullivan Gallery... in New York.

"Here are the coordinates." Christina said to the operator.

She relayed the name and number.

"Remember to remind Mister Sullivan that this is a radio phone call, and that everyone can listen and reply!"

New York! Maktu tried to imagine the scene where Mr. Sullivan sat. It really was marvellous that a person who lived so deep in Nature to get a call from New York. Maktu saw clearly the absurdity of a man who lives alone in the wilderness creating works of art that a New York gallery might want to show... and hopefully sell!

"I've got your party on the line... go ahead."

After a number of busses and switch-connections, a male voice came over the speaker in Christina's cabin

"Maktu! I'm so glad you called." There was a pause. "Do you still want to have a show in New York? For my entire collection of winter's work?" Maktu asked, marvelling at how fast, it was now coming together after such a disastrous accident.

"Isn't that commonplace for the north." Brandon laughed. He knew the North from salmon. In fact, it all started when he saw some of Maktu's work in Whitehorse and later when he saw the full collection of that year's paintings from photos Christina had made and forwarded.

After cordialities, Maktu spoke first. "Mr. Sullivan, let me get this straight. From your latest fax, I understand you are still offering me a show that includes, airfare for me and a companion, plus expenses and a roof over our heads. Is that right?"

"That's the offer." Said Brandon

"How would I get them to you?"

"By air freight." He answered.

Their settings could not be more different. For Maktu it was a brilliant dawn across a lake surrounded by snow shrouded mountains, and except for the odd raven following the shoreline, it was silent.

For Brandon, except for the low ambient music of Haydn, sheltered from the mayhem just meters away by triple soundproof triple-paned windows. His office was surrounded by expensive art. On his desk was a picture of himself holding a huge 25lb. salmon. While on the other side of the continent, Maktu was having smoke salmon for breakfast.

"How are you?"

"Thanks to a wonderful public nurse and my dog," he scuffed Shag with his foot, "I'm alive, not as handsome as I once was, but I'm very much alive!" He smiled at Christina.

“Wonderful!” Said the gallery owner. “I received your photographs of this year’s pieces, and I want to discuss with you about me hosting a show here in New York and as soon as possible before you dump them in the lake again!” Brandon teased.

“Is that last Winter’s work that you sent photos of?”

“I don’t have anything else, and as you know, it is a miracle that I even have those.” Replied Maktu. There was a long pause

“I think you have great talent, and I’d like to have a presentation of all of your paintings that you sent the pictures of. Are they still available? I’ll pay for shipping from Whitehorse to New York.” He paused.

“Also, as I see it, the show would run for a month, and I’ll cover the promotion and, if you are available, I would also cover the travel expenses for you and your companion to come here for the opening. Alone, New York would eat you alive”.

“One thing I have to ask.” said Maktu “With all your generosity, what is your commission? Your slice of the pie, so to speak?”

“The gallery rate is 40% of sales and as noted, we cover all expenses and promotion. Needless to say, the price we will set on your paintings will be high, so I think you will do very well financially.”

Before Maktu could respond that it was certainly acceptable, a different voice cut in. “That doesn’t sound acceptable!” Came the voice over the phone. “Here Maktu goes out into the wilderness in the dead of winter whereas you know from his experiences of late, many things go wrong and you’ll take 35%? That does not sound acceptable!”

A third voice, a woman’s had entered into the conversation.

“Oh my God!” Maktu exclaimed to himself. He’d forgotten to warn Brandon that they were talking on a ‘radiophone’, which meant it was a public broadcasting system.

“Yah, what about the commission?!” Came another woman’s voice.

“Oh MY GOD!” Christina shrieked with laughter. “You’d better explain that you are on a radiophone, and that everyone in the Yukon can hear your conversation... and... contribute to it!”

Brandon was startled by as yet another voice out of nowhere and his first thought was either the Federal Bureau of Investigation, or the Internal Revenue Service. Though neither alternative made any sense

“OK, Ok,” came a Native woman’s voice. “But what about the commission?”

“Yeah, what about the commission?” Came as yet another demanding voice across the wavelengths. “How much of the pie is going to Maktu?”

“Who is this?” Brandon asked, dumb founded by the interjection.

“This is Lillian!” She said matter-of-factly as if Brandon should recognise her voice. “Yeah. What about the commission?” Came another woman’s voice

“Oh my God!” Maktu started laughing, realising that Brandon didn’t understand that the call was on radiophone and broadcasted over most of the north-west and readily heard by everyone in the North who woke up to the day, made their first cup of coffee and turned on the radio-phone for entertainment.

Still, for his part, Brandon did understand the situation after years of salmon fishing in the far north. In fact, he was laughing so hard he had to cover the receiver with his hand until finally he caught himself.

“Well,” he got control, realising that the conversation had many participants. “Usually, the artist and I agree on a commission that is a percentage of the sale price."

"Hello Sir, this is Margret," A new voice cut in. "And just how much is that?"

"Yea, how much is that?" Came as yet a new voice.

"Who am I talking too now," inquired Brandon

"I'm sorry, sir. This is Mousada Tashoots".

"Well, Miss.Tashoots, we cover all expenses for the presentation in the gallery, plus hanging of the show and setting up lightening, plus media coverage like interviews on both television, radio, and the computer networks.

And then on the actual opening day of the show, we host a premier night with food and drinks, usually champagne. And of course there's publicity, advance press coverage, usually an artist interview on at least one National television show."

"Okay, okay ... so let's cut the chase. What's the bottom line?" Asked Mrs Tashoots.

But, before Brandon could answer he was hit by another question.

"OK, that's all and good, but what about where they're going to stay?"

"Yeah," Mrs Tashoots cut in again. "Should they bring a tent? If they camp in that Central Park, aren't they going to need a tent?"

"And what about bear protection?" Said Mrs. Kaskana.

"I understand that the airplane folks won't let you carry even a shotgun on board... can you imagine?!"

"Yah," Cut in Mrs Tashoots once more. "If there's going to be problems with a gun, maybe they should bring Shag. He's a great bear dog, ya know. He'll put the run on any bear even those in your town dump... and by the way, what is the name of the village where you are?"

By now Brandon was laughing so hard, Marlo had to take the phone away from him.

"Hello," a woman with a west coast accent cut in. "This is Marlo, I'm Mister Brandon's Assistant. To answer your question, 'Manhattan' The 'town' is called called 'Manhattan'... near Brooklyn."

Brandon took a drink of water and a deep breath and recovered himself. "But I fear you don't understand, we will reserve a room for them in a hotel for the duration of their stay."

There was a window of a silence before Mrs Kyoka spoke up, "Das good." Being the oldest Native matron of the village of K'sewet and considered one of the "Smart People", the subject was sealed, the phone was quiet for a moment.

"Well?" Mrs. Kyoka asked finally.

"Well, what?" Brandon asks.

"How much of a commission are you going to take if he decides to accept your offer for a show?" There is a long pause before she spoke again. "What did you say your Village is called?"

"Manhattan!" Maktu spoke up completely enjoying the conversation.

"Yeah, 'Manhattan'. But should they bring Shag.?.. he's put the run on a lot of bears trying to break into Maktu's food cache."

"No. we have bear-dogs here... they're called Chihuahuas and Poodles!"

"Okay..." Came as yet another new voice into the conversation. "Let's cut to the chase. How much of the pie are you going to take?"

"Our Gallery's rate is 40% of sales and that covers all expenses. But for Maktu I'll lower it to 35%"

"WHAT!" Exclaimed as yet a different voice. "Hell, and Damnation!! He can make more money painting barns!"

After all the haggling which Brandon was enjoying fully, he finally said, “25% and we will cover the expense of a tent, firewood and bear dog.”

“Take it!” Maktu yelled into the radiophone. “Yes, Mister Sullivan, I will accept that you get a twenty five percent commission, and you will cover everything.”

No one argued. Both Maktu, Christina and especially Brandon had enjoyed the interchange thoroughly. In truth, Maktu would have accepted Brandon’s cut much higher, it was all such an unexpected turn of events.

The gallery owner also had a wonderful time on the radiophone. “OK ... OK. But then we will have to cut back on our firewood cache and wear more sweaters this Winter, but you drive a hard bargain... all of you!”

“WAIT! What about residual expenses?” Came as yet another unknown voice. “I’ve heard you can go broke taking a cab from the airport to downtown Manhattan.”

“I’ll send my personal car and driver to pick them up at the Airport.”

The radiophone went silent for a minute before Maktu finally came on again. “Sounds great!” He too was laughing. “But maybe from now on we should communicate via the Internet. It’s a lot less crowded... and likely won’t cost you as much money.”

Brandon hung up the phone. There were tears in his eyes from repressed laughter.

Marlo looked at him sternly. “Can we afford this?” She asked when Brandon hung up.

“At any price.” He smiled. “This man’s work is brilliant! You look at it and you’ll thoroughly understand his importance. It would be a travesty to not help him every step of the way.”

Marlo stared at him, astonished, she had never heard him

speak with such enthusiasm.

“He doesn’t paint subjects, he paints ‘essences’. He is an original, and honestly, I consider it a privilege to represent him.”

“The Gallery may have to cut back on our ‘firewood allotment’ and wear heavy sweaters!” He laughed. “But this show will bring more attention to the Gallery than any other we have had... including Warhol!”

Chapter 16

By the time they landed at Kennedy International Airport it was well after dark. The flight across the continent from Vancouver to New York had been transformative for Maktu who had never crossed a single Time Zone, nor even been in a plane or helicopter that held more than two passengers and a dog.

On the flight from Whitehorse to Vancouver in a Boeing 737 Maktu was awestruck! First by the size of the airplane, and then the number of complete strangers with which he was confined. But it only lasted a short while until Christina anticipated his feelings and soon got him to focus on the view of the Coastal Range out the window and the view beneath them of a vast corridor of mountains capped by great blue glaciers with thin tendrils condensing into rivers reaching to the West and the Pacific coast, and as they approached Vancouver drifting to the East and the blue/green forest that soon evolved into ranch land and farms, then suddenly a city!

"Have faith." Christina whispered to Maktu as they began their descent into Vancouver Airport. "I'm sure the pilots have done this landing many times.....I hope!" She smiled.

"Pilots!" Thought Maktu, tightening his already firm grip on Christina's hand. "Wasn't just one enough!" He'd never been in a situation where more than one pilot was required... preferably

Chris.

"Give thanks!" Was an expression Chris used to say when his helicopter settled onto its skids and the rotors were stalled into a slow rap.

"Give thanks!" He whispered with awe when miraculously they collected their bags from a machine with conveyor belts that circled with many suitcases, and finally their bags.

"Give thanks!" He whispered when, with Christina in the lead, they threaded through waves of moving humans, more than he'd ever seen in a single place. Christina led him to another location in the airport where they stood in line to trust another complete stranger with his borrowed suitcase full of borrowed clothes.

The new plane from Vancouver to New York was huge! Maktu was terrified, imagining scenarios where they were all in a fearful situation – a stampede. Fortunately, Christina spoke with a stewardess who let them board last and because they were in First Class after take-off, she invited them to go up to the Boeing 747's upper lounge which had an overhead glass canopy.

It was dusk when the giant plane finally lumbered to the end of their assigned runway, turned and roared up its engines until Maktu's' ears hurt.

Suddenly, they lurched forward, the engines roared, gaining more and more volume. Then, just when Maktu feared they would run out of land and into the ocean, the nose of the beast rose up above the land and into the sky.

They flew West out over the Pacific Islands for a short while, then once away from the city and well above it and the surrounding mountains, they turned back to the East above Vancouver, then straightened out all the while gaining altitude.

"We're going on an adventure." Smiled Christina.

The sun was setting behind them in the West, its rays

igniting the mountains below and ahead. Finally mesmerised by the magnificence of the view of the spectacular sunset, he relaxed his grip on Christina's arm.

"We're going on an adventure!" Christina repeated, squeezed his hand and gave him a reassuring smile.

Once away from the Lower Mainland Valley, and the checker-board farmland turned into the vertical polish granite walls of the Rockies which also became ignited by the setting sun behind and, as far as he could see ahead it was a vast stretch of flatland.

Only then as the plane levelled did Maktu realise that he had been holding his breath, all the while squeezing Christina's hand even harder!

"Look up!' Christina whispered. There directly above, visible through the 747's glass canopy was a full moon!

It was when they crossed the East slope of the Rockies into Alberta, when he spotted the odd droplets of light presumably farms. And soon thin streams of car lights emerged, yellow and white going one way and red lights the other.

The droplets of white lights flowing at them merged with red lights going the opposite direction. Also, the first white puddles of stationary lights eventually merged into ponds of rural farm towns and soon they swelled into lakes of lights. Maktu looked at Christina quizzically as the lakes became eventually an ocean.

He looked up at the moon.

"Do you think man has flown to the moon?" Christina asked Maktu.

He thought about the question. "Of course!" He said it as if the answer were obvious.

"Why do you think that?" She asked.

"If Mankind can fly at all...why not to the moon!" He replied.

For a long time Maktu sat fascinated with the cascades and

clusters of lights below. And the further East they flew, the streams of lights grew into wide rivers flowing in both directions..., one going one way, one the other.

"It makes no sense. If the folks over there," he nodded to the flow of cars coming from the West, "if they just did the tasks that those people who are going the way we came from do," he nodded to the flow coming from the East, it would save a lot of time in a car." He grinned. "And everybody could just stay at home!"

Then he laughed. "It is all a conspiracy to sell gas!".

Suddenly, a huge cluster of lights sprung up out of the Eastern landscape swallowing the incoming and out-going lights into a lake of solid light!

"Calgary" The stewardess smiled.

And soon, the further East they flew, the ponds became more lakes of lights. which the stewardess knew the name of each.

"Regina," She'd say, then."Winnipeg", "Toronto..." Not once using a map.

Finally, the landscape below them became one solid mass of incandescence, and stranger still, as they descended, Maktu felt the landscape was coming up around them and even the moon seemed to be an intruder. In fact, he felt like an intruder descending into a landscape of vertical surfaces and a shrinking sky.

"New York?" He asked the flight attendant.

"Yes...would you like something else?" She asked then, when he shook his head no, she reached across and gently pried his hand locked in a death-grip off the 'Call' button.

"I wish Shag could see this." He muttered to the Christina.

"You'll have to remember it and tell him all about it when you get home." Said Christina.

"Shag?" Asked the Stewardess.

"He's a friend." Christina smiled.

"He's a friend who saved my life." Maktu began his story but suddenly he became terrified as the airport landing lights raced up at them from below.

"Are we under attack?" Asked Mattu terrified. .

When the stewardess explained that they were actually "Landing" in New York and not in fact being assaulted by 'aliens' from a different planet from below, he once again relaxed his grip on Christina's wrist.

"However," said the stewardess, "some say New York is a different Planet,"

"First flight over New York?" The stewardess said pointing to Maktu to buckle his seatbelt.

"It's his first flight over any place that isn't home to mountain goats and tree squirrels." Christina smiled.

"Where are you from?"

"Western Canada... now." Christina replied. "But before I was raised in Pennsylvania".

"Funny," the stewardess observed, "I feel the same way you do about flying into Vancouver with all the gorgeous mountains clawing holes in the sky!"

As they exited the plane, Maktu was not convinced that they hadn't just risen up and the Earth turned underneath them, instead of them going down until they exited at a concourse and they were confronted by crowds of people, moving through the terminal, Being a Native Indian and thus not having a beard, protecting most of his face he suddenly, for the first time, since his accident on the lake felt self- conscious about his special mountaineering glasses and his special leather gloves that he wore to protect his damaged hands, but where grafts were necessary,

Even though she was once a seasoned traveller at the JFK Airport, even Christina suddenly became anxious. In all of the confusion of moving the man who was a virgin to the adultery of modern travel, and especially in a crowded airport, the confusion of reading flight times and baggage-claim terminals, plus having to go from from terminal to terminal with a man who was in complete awe; she felt anxious.

Also, she hadn't made arrangements with the Sullivan Gallery for getting from the airport to their hotel, wherever that was. Hopefully they would get a driver who knew New York. All she had was the name, "Park Lane" but no address. She had been to New York many times, growing up outside of Philadelphia, but always with an address to her destination.

"Maktu!... Christina!" Came a loud voice from a young man in his mid-twenties wearing Levis and a cowboy hat.

"Cowboy Bob," he introduced himself

As soon as he saw Maktu's bandages and thick dark glasses, he had immediately recognised them and turned to Christina and helped her pull their bags from the carousal.

After quick introductions, they went out into the brilliant incandescent night of the City and Bob guided them sleekly through the carnival of cabs picking up passengers.

He spoke to the driver of the front car, and they got in.

Maktu didn't speak during the drive into the Hotel. He was awe struck!

At one point Christina asked Cowboy Bob. "Wouldn't it be faster if we took the Eastside Parkway?"

The driver looked in his rear mirror, startled that she knew New York well enough to have an informed opinion.

She smiled. "A perverted youth in a girls-school in Bryn Mawr, Pennsylvania.... New York was our escape." Christiana confessed to Maktu, grinning. Secretly she was pleased to be back in the jungle of humanity.

"When I'm in the bush," Maktu said to her, "the mountains and the lakes, the animals and the birds are all familiar! But here nothing is as it should be."

"That's why it's called New York." Laughed the cab driver, everything is new every day!"

"Scared?" Christina asked, squeezing his hand.

"Nope..." He smiled. "I've decided to become a 'sponge', and just take it all in. Absorb it all! My 'mantra', as you say, is to 'absorb' and take in as much as I can... and that is what I am going to do."

"Where you from buddy?" Asked the driver

"So far back in the mountains that even the wolves have to pack a lunch to get there." Christina joked.

"I know the place!" Laughed the cabbie. "But our wolves here wear suits and they will eat anything!" He grinned, as the cab pulled over to the curb in front of a lavish hotel.

Maktu looked across the street. "How civilised to put a Park in the middle of a city."

"It's called 'Central Park' and there are no bears... though plenty of predators!" Laughed Cowboy Bob.

Christina left Maktu and Bob in the lobby and went directly to the Check-in Desk. Maktu started to pay the driver who stared at the strange money and refused the multi-coloured Canadian bills in sharp contrast to all green American currency.

Bob paid the fare.

Maktu had been told by the lawyer Brand that usually when you get a ride in Manhattan in a taxi, you should give the driver a tip.

Maktu shook hands with him, and demonstrating he was not a complete hick from the far continental Northwest, he put his good arm around the driver's shoulder and for a tip he said, "It's going to be a good Spring! Plant your crops early!" And gave him a generous smile.

Bob slipped the driver a twenty, who muttered loudly and squealed away from the curb.

Christina joined them, a little confused and bewildered.

"The desk clerk just told me that the Gallery is covering our stay! Room, meals, everything. And", she grinned at Maktu, "the Gallery owner, Mister Sullivan, would like to see you first thing in the morning!"

Their room was at the top of the Hotel and had a wrap-around view of the City lights... everywhere except a startling dark quiet view out onto a forest of trees nestled amongst an otherwise horizon of lights reaching well into the sky.

"It's called Central Park!" Christina smiled.

Though exhausted, Maktu couldn't sleep, absently wondering if he'd hear the owls in the morning announcing a new dawn that he was accustomed to.

Chapter 17

"You sure?" Maktu asked the cabbie as they pulled up in front of a red brick old bank building, dwarfed in a forest of tall, thirty story structures of glass: their entrances firmly planted at ground-level and guarded by doormen in uniforms.

His destination was a two and a half story red brick building on a concrete foundation, the entrance of which was a set of a large spacious stairs guarded on each side by concrete lions.

"You sure?" Maktu asked again.

"Buddy... the Brandon Sullivan Fine Art Gallery has been here since before my Daddy started driving hacks... That'll be $20 plus tip."

Maktu laboriously pulled his wallet from the inside pocket of his borrowed jacket where he'd wedged it to thwart the pickpockets that he'd been cautioned about back in Lone Bull. He looked inside. Hidden amongst the colourful Canadian bills, he found a green twenty-dollar U.S. bill and handed it to the cabbie.

"And here's your tip." He leaned forward towards the driver. "Plant your crops early this year, I'm told it is going to a good year... an early Spring".

He grinned, tapped the man on the shoulder, stepped away quickly as the cab leapt forward. He doubted the cabbie would take his advice, Maktu shrugged, more likely he didn't even have a garden. .

After climbing the tier of deeply worn concrete steps, watching the lions closely, half expecting their eyes would open with flashing lights and an artificial growl would follow. "Expect anything, in New York" was Christina's final advice as he walked out of their hotel.

At the top of the stairs was a polished brass plated sign that read:

.

"Sullivan Fine Art Gallery"

Maktu took a deep breath, he'd feared this moment ever since he left Lone Bull. Somehow if his show was in a huge skyscraper where everyone would rush by it would be preferable, but in a real art gallery where people come specific to look at his art, study it and comment.

But, as Christina said as he left the Hotel,"You've faced worst. I would go with you if I thought you'd be torn apart. But there are no grizzly bears in New York– you've faced worse."

Once he did have to shoot an angry grizzly, reluctantly, but the bear was intent on destroying his camp – and presumably him when he was finished with the pots and pans and the tents. But that was nothing to facing a herd of humans. If his show would be in a glass building of elevators and doormen and herds of people not looking and judging his work, he could accept that. In fact, he'd prefer that to an intimate viewing with a gracious hostess who would offer to show his paintings that were in a bright well light room, and a well-practised spiel of platitudes about the 'special' light of the "Great Canadian North" and how someday she hoped to go there.

Contrary to his fears, the inside entrance to Sullivan Gallery led into a large round rotunda with a vaulted arched ceiling that opened to the sky two stories above. The walls were carved wood-panels, each with a single painting illuminated by focused lights shining just upon them.

"May I help you?" Asked a tall woman dressed in a soft summer dress that seemed to be designed just for her. She came around the desk and extended her hand.

Maktu noticed a stack of photos on the desk and realised that they were of his collection. There was one picture with "Cover" written upon it.

The woman followed his gaze and picked up the pictures. "It will be the front cover for this show. What do you think?"

He smiled, it was in fact his favourite painting in the collection; a pastel sunset, with a single bead of the retreating sun just below the horizon washing the entire setting in lavenders and golds.

"And you must be Mister..." She paused for a moment not sure if Maktu was his first or last name.

"Yes. ... Maktu." He took her extended hand. "Both first and last. My birth name name is "Da-de-ta-wana" which is my Native family name. But I am known only as Maktu," he grinned.

"And you are?" He extended his hand.

She blushed but quickly regained her poise. "My name is Marlo!" Her smile was radiant when they shook hands.

She thought to herself that she had never been in contact with a person of such a strong presence, even confidence. Yes, that was it... hard, callused hands, and tender inquisitive and confident eyes.

"Mr. Sullivan has been waiting for you." She leaned over her desk and pushed a button on the intercom and a moment later a door opened above at the top of a set of circular stairs.

"Welcome!" Boomed a man's voice. "We've been expecting

you."

He nodded to the woman. "You have met Marlo?" He paused for a moment. "You will soon discover, she runs this place! I just pay the bills."

The woman blushed.

"Come ... come!" He waved to a curved staircase leading up to where he stood.

"Brandon," he extended his hand. "Brandon Sullivan." Maktu extended his right hand, hoping that Brandon would not notice that his left hand was in a black leather glove.

The inside of Brandon's office, in keeping with the entrance rotunda, was curved with paintings in an oasis of cubicles of individual paintings, each with their own lighting, most with built in ceiling lights.

"Oh my God!" Maktu exclaimed as he scanned the room! Salted amongst the collection of, he presumed, well known artists, there were a half-dozen of his works... paintings that he had displayed at the Yukon Hotel and the airport in Whitehorse, with discrete signs that read "Not for Sale". Obviously, they were part of the Gallery owner's private collection. Also, there were the two very large canvases from the Whitehorse Airport which Maktu had reluctantly had on display thinking they'd never sell given their size and price.

"You flatter me." Was all Maktu could say

"You humble me." Said Brandon

"Coffee?" Said the gallery owner as Marlo entered with a tray. They each took a cup.

"So here is the schedule. As you know the show's opening is tomorrow night, Saturday. Marlo and I have done a tentative hanging of the paintings which, when we finish our coffee, we can can go around and you can make suggestions about lighting and placements. Nothing is fixed in stone if you want changes." He looked at Maktu.

"Also, I've taken the liberty of inviting the Art Columnist from the 'New York Times', who will be here momentarily to see the show and meet you for her column this Sunday morning in the Weekend Edition."

"Also, I've arranged a television interview tomorrow morning."

"I've never been interviewed." Maktu confessed.

"You'll do fine. Just be yourself."

"I don't think that is a good idea!" Maktu had only seen a television in a store window in Whitehorse and ironically what was playing was an episode of "Sergeant Preston of the Yukon and His Wonder Dog, King!"

"So, now bring your coffee, I want to show you the Show's arrangement that Marlo and I spent yesterday, and into last night laying out... subject, of course, to your approval." He looked at his watch. "Let's go before Angela Walton, the *Times* columnist arrives".

"Also," he added "Marlo called your hotel and spoke with Christina about going clothes shopping this afternoon, and I thought it would be a good idea for you and I to do the same." That suited Maktu just fine as he wondered what to wear for a gallery show in the City.

Then, almost as an afterthought, Brandon reached across his desk and picked up an envelope and handed it to Maktu. "It is a copy of the contract. Twenty five percent commission... as 'negotiated'", he stressed the word with a smile by your 'agents' plus an advance so you can pick up any necessities, while you're here."

Maktu was pleased with the advance, there were things to get, one in particular that he wanted to pick-up in New York and that necessitated a trip, as Brand advised, to Tiffany's!

The Gallery design was a series of interconnecting rooms one leading to the next around the two storey central mezzanine. Maktu was impressed. The entire gallery featured exclusively his works with an inner dispersion of sizes, arranged by subject. The large paintings commanded their own walls, while the smaller ones were dispersed so they actually seemed to stand alone which was the consequence of individual lighting, and in some cases, the subject matter. One small painting that commanded a cubicle of its own was a painting of a single, hanging pinecone with ice crystals dripping from its seedpods, each droplet a multi-coloured collage of diamonds. In the rotunda three very large paintings had a wall to themselves, each with their own lighting.

The opening painting to the show, the one featured on the brochure cover was a large canvas, a signature piece of a sunrise casting the fire from a morning Northern dawn upon the crowns of surrounding mountain peaks. On the opposite wall were the same mountains caught in a blue lavender sunset.

Throughout the show there was an orderly development, as the entire show evolved from dawn to dusk, each piece featuring an aspect of Maktu's unique handling of northern light.

"I'm impressed." Said Maktu when they'd finished the tour and returned to Brandon's office ,"I'm very impressed that you can make my work look so good!"

"With your work it is easy. "

He paused for a moment, and it was obvious that there was more he wanted to say. "But" Maktu blurted out, "I just wonder how you can make a living selling paint slapped on canvas!" He blurted out, then shyly smiled.

Just then Marlo came in and freshened their coffee.

Brandon filled Maktu's cup and his own, took a sip, smiled and replied. "Ah my friend, it is how the paint is 'slapped' on the canvas."

They each smiled at the truism, but both remained silent again, each studying the other.

"Why...?" Maktu suddenly blurted out. "Why have you gone to the trouble to do all this .. collecting and showing so much of my work? And then searching me out and bringing me all this way?" He shook his head as if the reality that he had come from where he was just a week ago to here, from an extremely isolated region on the shores of a very remote lake in the Canadian wilderness. He waved his gloved hand to include the entire room... then he leaned forward engaging Brandon's eyes with his question, "... and giving me a stand-alone show in your obviously very important gallery." .

Brandon smiled. "..., ah... a man straight to the point." He took a deep drink of coffee and leaned back in his chair. "I like that... and frankly I would expect no less from you." He looked directly at Maktu.

"Why?" Well, the answer is authenticity. It is the 'Great North' captured in all of its faces and dimensions into a single image".

Maktu was not satisfied. "I'm sorry if I am being rude, but my question again, how can you make a living selling pieces of canvas with paint slathered on them?" Maktu smiled, though only half-heartedly. In his mind, work and wages were grounded on either labour or tangible goods, ... but selling other people's artistic endeavours seemed a dangerous way of making a living. Maktu felt embarrassed that he had put it so bluntly, but it was a question that had lingered in his mind from his very first sale of a painting back when his art was on worn-out tent canvas and house paint.

Brandon leaned forward. "Art is an indulgence not a necessity!" He looked intently at Maktu. "Foremost art, be it a painting, a ballet, or a music concerto, is a window into a special side of the soul... the human Creative Spirit."

"And it is not limited to art, music, dance. even the architecture of skyscrapers is nutrition for the creative side of the soul. It is the soul seeking ways to find release. It's a quest that starts from the baby's first need to express itself beyond the pragmatism of survival."

Brandon looked across the room at a portrait painting by someone Maktu did not recognise. "My father told me," Continued Brandon, "that the pursuit of the creative urge, either as a creator or a witness is to simply connect people with that need."

"Art is the consequence of the senses translating our tangible lives into the emotive... and sometimes even the spiritual views."

Maktu was floored by the observations, but he knew that would be fuel for further thought.

"You see, I am neither a creator, nor a scribe but when I come across someone who is, I celebrate them for showing me something I may not have ever seen were it not for them."

"So, if, as in your case, if I can enable a person to continue with their pursuit, that is my reward. If I can take a chance and make money for both of us so much the better."

"You know, effective art in its many faces changes our perspective of the outside world. Great art does this indelibly!"

He thought for a moment. "I fear I have over answered your question, but I have a story that might help you understand why I support people 'slathering' paint on canvas."

"Good art takes the soul on a journey. And sometimes it is a journey once travelled we want more. Also, once travelled it leads to seeking more. And you can never go back... you can never un-experience it!"

"Music is an art form. It is a form that can transcend moments of a dull present and move people to dance around or close their eyes and leave the material moment and be moved dance in their imagination, to liberate them from the confines of their being. And art can be indelible and once you have experienced core.... the 'essence' of something, as my father said, "You can never go back to the mundane!"

Maktu was bewildered.

"Here," Brandon leaned forward. "Let me give you an example. One time I saw a large Monet painting of a field of poppies. Sometime later, in my mid-youth, maybe twenty, I was on a train in France and saw out the window a brilliant explosion of poppies in a field and I was immediately reminded of Monet's painting. But moreover ... in fact, the experience was indelible because, having seen the painting I saw immediately the essences of the subject! And... I will never forget it!"

His eyes lit up. "That is what art does. It shows us, filtered through the artist, be they be a painter, a poet, a composer, or a dancer, they relive the essence of a subject." He leaned forward, "and in a way that we can never unsee it!"

"That is what I do! I offer people art that moves their souls, their moods, perspectives enough that they want to live with it."

He paused and took a drink of coffee. "That is what your paintings do for me, and I'm betting that others will feel the same." He looked around the walls of his office. "I do not sell art, as say a person might sell a washing machine, or a television. What I offer are triggers for the imagination that are so strong that one can not see the subject without remembering the artist's rendition of it."

He had been leaning back in his chair as he spoke but suddenly, he rocked forward. "I'm betting that what your work does for me, will touch others... simple as that."

He looked long at Maktu, "That's what I do, I offer people a window, an experience without having to go there to the North in sub-zero temperatures to experience it."

He then laughed. "Also, I think 'great art' should be transformative so that you can never see the subject the same way after seeing or hearing it filtered through the artist."

"So", he again rocked back in his chair, "to answer your question. Selling art, is selling windows for the imagination to play with. Great art is never seeing the subject without experiencing the art-form of it. That's what I do!"

Brandon looked at his watch. "The Times reporter will be here soon, and I have a schedule for us before the show. Anyway, that's why you are here. I'm betting... no, I'm gambling that other people are going to feel the same."

He let the ideas settle on Maktu then snapped forward and looked at a calendar on his desk.

"I've taken the liberty of scheduling for you and I to do a little shopping this afternoon and get you some clothes that suit who you are, so you aren't having to borrow. Also, Marlo and Christina have arranged to do some shopping for a 'special' dress for the show.

"That would be good." Maktu smiled. "I too have something I want to pick up."

Their conversation was interrupted by Marlo on the intercom, "Mrs. Walton from the New York Times is here."

Brandon turned to Maktu, "If you don't mind, I'll give her a tour of the show before she meets you." And with that, Brandon went out of the office and closed the door. Maktu for his part used the time to study the Gallery owner's private collection.

"I'm flattered, but I can't imagine what I could say to an art columnist." He said to Marlo who was arranging some papers.

"You'll have no problems."

When Brandon and Mrs. Walton finished the tour, the door

opened and Maktu met an older woman carrying a very well-worn brief case on a shoulder strap. He had the feeling that she had been with the New York Times for a long time and probably had done hundreds of interviews with artists. Still, she seemed interested to meet Maktu.

"Be gentle on him." Brandon laughed on his way out of his office. . "He is but a 'child of the wilderness'!" He said smiling as he closed the door behind him.

Her first question was boilerplate, "Where did you study?"

Maktu was set back and a little embarrassed.

"Well, to tell you the truth Mam. I am an imitator. I just paint what I see. I've never had lessons. And if the subject-matter for a painting is where my 'soul abides' as, my Grandmother would say, it is easy to make the transition into my paintings".

She scratched in her notes "Where the soul abides."

He thought for a moment. "To answer your question about where did I learn to paint? I've never had lessons other than what my 'Gran' taught me. You see, I was raised by my Grandparents. My immediate family, my mother, father, older brother and a younger sister were all killed in a head-on car crash by a drunk – in, fact he was my cousin... he also died immediately."

Maktu fell silent for a moment, then smiled looking at the floor, he felt surprisingly comfortable with the woman. "You know what kills Indians?" He laughed looking up. "It is not defending the Lone Ranger... it is mixing gasoline and alcohol at 90 miles/hour! That's what kills Indians!" The journalist sensed his anger, but it quickly passed.

"Anyway," he looked up, "to answer your question, I had been left with my Grands and they lived in a very remote tribal village so far back in the mountains that the road, what there was of it, was only open to vehicles in the Spring to early fall, and after that you had to snowshoe, snowmobile or take a dog team in.

When the Mounties came into notify us about the accident, they came in by helicopter. I was very young, but I still remember the helicopter... but I only vaguely remember my Father and Mother and siblings!" He looked at his hands for a long time. then returned to the interview.

"My Grandmother loved drawing and painting pictures when she could get or make paints... and find clear paper or scraps of canvas. But she taught me with what she had. I do remember she bought me a watercolour set from the money they made selling fox and beaver pelts that Grandpa trapped... but most of my first drawings were on cardboard." He laughed.

"When she saw that I had some interest, and maybe even talent, she bought me a small oil-paint set at the Hudson Bay Company store in Whitehorse. Also, she got me some 8"x10" canvases that came in a tear out folder."

"Oh..." Maktu remembered, "and an old torn tent some people had thrown away, that we cut into painting sizes and stretched it with apple box slates. For paints I collected near-empty house-paint cans from the Whitehorse dump."

Mrs. Walton looked at him incredulously. "Was he making this up?" She wondered.

"No, it is all true. Maybe that's why I paint with soft colours. Back then they painted their homes with bright pastel colours." He laughed. "No... my first attempts were house paints on cardboard or sometimes worn-out canvas."

He thought for a moment. "When I started doing odd jobs for people in the Village and had a little money I bought regular artist's oil paints, but I still sometimes stretch my own canvases out of old tent canvases...." He laughed.

He thought for a moment. "Also, because my Grands still lived their heritage, and I was raised by them in a small settlement with only seasonal accessibility by a drivable road and it still only came part way in to the village in the Winter, I wasn't, at first, exposed to the regular public schools and therefore I've never had any formal art lessons".

"Fortunately, Granny could read and do figures, and she insisted I learn to do the same."

"But," he said after a moment's thought. "Granny always said about painting, "Let the subject tell you how to paint it." And I guess that is what I still do, I try to capture not just what the eye sees but also..." He paused searching for a word... "the 'essence' of the subject! And that's what a pilot friend named Chris told me too. He told me to paint the 'feeling' of it, what makes it live and what is interesting to me, and hopefully that's what others see." He fell silent for a moment. "So, that's what I paint... my feelings."

There was a silence between them then Maktu spoke again. "I guess, being raised without the distractions of having other kids around, or other amusements like movies and television, I turned my attention to painting."

"The magazines Gran brought home from her occasional trips out for supplies, gave me ideas for subjects to explore. But Gran was of the opinion that you paint what you feel... and not just what you see". He thought for a long time. "In truth, I am an imitator. I imitate something, ... usually a 'feeling' in Nature by filtering it through my paint brush". He fell silent for a moment, thinking.

"It is mainly the light! A camera can capture the form of a subject and to some extent the light, but I dissect the light into elements, and for me, the success of a painting, the power of it, is the light. The subject is the body, the light is ... how do you say, the soul!"

He thought for a moment, "I was recently told a story of how a painting of a field of poppies by the French artist Monet, captured the soul of the subject so well that when this person saw the real thing, he was reminded of the painting."

"That is what I aim for with my art... to reach beyond flowers in a field to their essences..." He thought of a phrase Brandon had used., "The transcendental".

"I try to paint what touches my soul, and once seen, it can never be unseen." He fell silent for a moment, thinking.

"Also, the light of the far North is so spectacular and uniquely breathtaking that basically I just try to imitate what is there. And honestly, when I capture it I don't need to enhance anything! I am not a painter; I am an imitator who paints!"

Mrs. Walton studied him with a measure of disbelief. "Was he bullshitting her... going from partly used buckets of house paints on cardboard, and torn tents to a feature show in the famed Sullivan Gallery?"

"You live by yourself on a remote lake in the Yukon?"

He nodded not sure if that was a good thing or not, but it was the truth.

Before she left the Gallery, she stopped in Brandon's office, ostensibly to pick up her purse, but she was still not convinced that Maktu was who he appeared.

"Brandon, are you pulling my journalistic leg? Am I correct, that you are doing a feature show in one of New York's most famous galleries, of a man's work who lives in the wilderness – and he has never taken a formal art lesson in his life ... and he started off with paint-ends of empty house paint cans and tent canvas?"

Brandon grinned. "Other than adding that his sole companion is his dog who recently saved his life, and had things gone ever so slightly the other way, he'd be dead! That's why he wears mountaineer glasses to protect skin grafts around his eyes, and a leather gloves to protect two missing fingers on his left hand ... and he is left-handed."

He smiled at her. “I asked him recently that question in an email and he wrote back via his girlfriend “My spirit abides in the Wild” and it’s so powerful that I am humbled to try to capture it with paints.” He thought for a moment.

“So, your answer is ‘yes’, he is authentic. “And,” he added, “I hope you will be doing him justice and that I think you have an accurate assessment of the man and his work.”

“Also, by his own admission, painting allows him to live, as he says, “where his soul abides”. In his view, he is just a scribe for what is around him and as he admits, he feels privileged for the experience”.

It was at this point that Maktu came into the office. “Oh, I’m sorry.” He apologised.

“Don’t you get lonely out there alone?” Asked Ms. Walton.

“Of course, you can only tell yourself the same joke so many times.”

She laughed.

“But I do believe I’ve met a woman who shares my love for Nature and my lifestyle away from humans.”

“Have you asked her to be your partner?”

He lowered his gaze to the floor. “No... I’m a cowardly man... I’d like to ask her, but I don’t have the courage.”

“Well, ... if she reads my column in this week’s Sunday Times Edition. You already have!”

There was a long silence as he thought about her words.

“Yep ... I guess I just did!” He grinned

She glanced at her notes, reflected on what she saw on the tour of his paintings and the interview. She realised that he was not putting her on, he was exactly as he came across, a gentle soul at home with natural beauty and silence that she could only imagine and envy.

When the interview was over, she rose, extended her hand and thanked him, but said nothing about the piece, or even if she got enough for an article.

She turned to Maktu, her hand on the doorknob.

"Remember to give a copy of my article in this Sunday Edition of the New York Times to your girlfriend." She gave him a big grin.

On her way out of the Gallery, she stopped and picked up her purse.

"Where is did you find him?"

"In the Canadian wildness." Brandon smiled. "Did you get your story?"

"You'll have to pick up a Weekend Edition of the Times." She smiled and left.

Brandon walked her to the Gallery's entrance.

"So, how did it go?" Brandon asked.

At the Gallery door Mrs. Walton smiled. "I thought when you said that you were having a feature showing of a completely unknown artist from the extreme 'Wilds of the Yukon'...someone who had never had a show in his life. I assumed that your age had finally caught up with you... now I am humbled by your insight."

"And" Brandon added. "Even if his work were ho-hum, the story of how he got out from the depths of the wilderness to our gallery is itself remarkable. It is right out of "Call of the Wild". And as a painter, his images are unforgettable. Now you see why I insisted that you come here in person."

"Well?" Maktu asked after Mrs. Walton left.

Brandon grinned. "I knew it would go well." He said.

"Now!" He said to Maktu. "What are you doing for lunch?"

"Also, I think we should get you some clothes that fit you." Brandon smiled.

"Lunch and maybe clothes shopping?"

Marlo called Christina at the Hotel and invited her to lunch.

"I'd like that very much!" Christina said enthusiastically. "Maktu just called and said he's having lunch with Brandon. Where should we meet? At the Gallery?"

"Perfect!" Said Marlo. "I could come and pick you up if you wish."

"Not necessary, I know New York intimately... I was raised in Bryn Mawr, Pennsylvania., and my girlfriends and I used to escape to the clubs in New York when we were still underage." She smiled. "It is a long story. I'll tell you over lunch."

Chapter 18

"We have choices." Said Brandon. "Abercrombie and Fitch, Brooks Brothers or Patagonia? I think you will find everything you'll need for the show."

Maktu didn't mention that none of his wardrobe was his and all of it was borrowed.

They went first to Abercrombie's. Maktu needed everything and the name or reputation of any of the stores meant nothing to him.

Brandon told the store's clerk the situation. For Maktu, even a pair of Levis and comfortable tennis shoes for touring the Central Park, would have been fine.

With Brandon's consultation, Maktu ended up with a tan suede sports jacket, light brown slacks, a powder blue shirt, tan leather shoes. Basically everything, a complete wardrobe for the occasion, except Maktu drew the line at a tie.

From Abercrombie's, they went up a few of blocks and over to an outdoors store called "Patagonia". This was more to Maktu's interest since all of the merchandise there was outdoor wear. But, as he immediately realised, it was lightweight! The heavy wolverine coat he wore when the temperature was -30 with a wind, weighed many pounds, while a sub-zero nylon and acrylic-fibre parka at Patagonia weighed but less than a pound!

Brandon had to insist that they leave after a half hour in the store. "You'll spend all of you painting sales-money in just one spot."

"I do have one more request." Maktu insisted. "A jewellery store. One with a global name that people in 'Timbuktu' will recognise. I have heard of your famous 'Tiffany Jewellery Store', I have a rather odd purchase I'd like to make there." Maktu grinned. "Is it close?"

Brandon guided him through the subway system. When they surfaced it was at the Rockefeller Center. Maktu had moved into a permanent state of awe, resigned to take in as much as he could, and sort out the details when he returned to the Canadian wild.

"What are you looking for?" Brandon asked.

"Just trust me. I may need an ally." Maktu smiled.

"Mister Singleton" Brandon said to the doorman dressed in a uniform of slacks, a long coat, gloves, and a tall hat, who stepped over to a phone by the door.

"Two gentlemen to see you Mister Singleton." He turned away from Brandon and Maktu and whispered into the phone, "I believe one is Mister Sullivan."

As they walked in Maktu was staggered by the explosion of lights. The store sparkled like the jewels it housed. There was very little sense of commercialism other than the cases with internal lights that made the gems they harboured sparkle.

"I will need your support with my request." Maktu said to Brandon.

"What and how much?" Brandon looked the artist, wondering what he would possibly need at Tiffany's. "My wallet is yours." He grinned.

"Hopefully it won't be necessary." Maktu smiled, still not giving away any information.

They stood but a moment by the door when a man in a grey suit and a white rose in his lapel, bustled up to them, his hand extended.

“Brandon! What a wonderful surprise! I haven’t seen you since your daughter’s graduation.”

They shook hands. “What can I do for you?”

“Well John, it is my friend here, he has a request. John, this is Maktu, a young painter I am exhibiting his work at the Gallery opening tomorrow. I hope you will come. He has a request. The two men shook hands. It will be a pleasure to attend to you.”

The Jeweller turned to Maktu.

“What can I do for you?”

“I need a box.” Maktu said.

“What kind of a box?” Both men were puzzled.

“A ring box with ‘Tiffany’ embossed on it.”

“Humm.” Said the store manager. “Normally we put something in them.”

“Nope, for now just a ring box with ‘Tiffany’ on it.”

Brandon looked away from Maktu to the Store’s manager and shrugged. “Surely you can part with a ring box with the store’s logo on it can’t you?” He smiled.

The manager grinned. “No problem. And tomorrow at your show,” he turned to Maktu, “maybe you can explain.” He left the two men and returned with a blue/black ring box with ‘Tiffany’s’ engraved on it.

“I look forward to your show and the explanation.”

En route back to the Gallery Maktu ducked into a cigar store where he bought two Cuban cigars both banded with a paper ring certifying their authenticity and that their origin was Cuba.

“Soon all will be explained.” He grinned and offered Brandon a cigar.

"I don't smoke."

"Neither do I, but it is my goal to to take in as much as I can while I'm here, and I've always wondered what the attraction of cigars was."

They crossed the street and sat down on a park bench.

"Go lightly. Cigars are pretty strong".

"How do I do it?"

"Light the flat end and just take a couple small puffs to get it going, and then if you're brave inhale and hold it for a second then blow it out... not in someone's face!"

****

Christina came back from her shopping spree with the help of Marlo. She was delighted with what she had found. It was exactly the dress she envisioned for the show.

Maktu started to reach for the dress-box and promptly got his hand slapped. "Tonight." She grinned.

However, in turn, she was very curious about Maktu's purchases, one of which he too kept boxed in an ordinary brown paper bag.

"What now?" Maktu asked.

Christina looked out the window. "The Park... let's go for a walk in Central Park".

Chapter 19

Maktu's face lit up with the idea of exploring the Park. "Yes. it would be too bad to come all the way to New York and not visit Central Park. After all it is just across the street."

As they walked, they were surprised how calm, even quiet it was in the middle of a city. The people around them were equally relaxed, actually strangers greeting strangers... in New York City, blatantly free of the turmoil around them.

"Look up!" Christina said, "That's our room at the top of the Hotel".

Maktu was amazed at how in the heart of the city you could be surrounded by calm, uncrowded and peaceful. Couples strolled holding hands comfortable in the presence of their partner. Birds flew, fluttered, fed on insects just as they did in the Yukon. Most were different species than he knew, but Maktu did recognised the ubiquitous robins and a few jays, even a raven... or was it a crow?

"Crow", Christina assured him, as she picked a few pieces of popcorn she'd purchased from a street vendor and threw them out to the bird.

"That's us." Christina smiled as they passed a young couple locked in the presence of the other's company – oblivious of others on the foot path.

"Oh my God!" Exclaimed Christina as a skunk waddled down the footpath towards them. "He's so cute." She knelt down assuming he was fixed since he was dragging a leash. Still, she expected the animal to turn and run away, but it instead it came waddling up to them and stopped in front of Christina and Maktu!.

"Don't panic." Came the voice of a man not far behind the skunk. "It's just his way of meeting people. The skunk's name Rosebud."

Then, just as a fat furry dog would do, it waddled up to her and rubbed against her leg. Christina opened her hand and the skunk saw the buttered popcorn! Christina made a distracting noise, shifted her weight slightly away from him, and when it looked away, she flipped the popcorn into the other hand. Sure enough, curiosity over-came him and after looking around, he nuzzled her other hand and found the popcorn there.

"You've made a friend... he loves games." Came a voice advancing towards them, from behind the skunk. The man wore the universal attire of a street person, a huge coat, a rumpled hat and gloves with missing fingers.

"Here, give him this." Said the man and offered them an open bag of peanuts.

"He acts like your pet... Is he?" Asked Christina.

"More like 'friend'. I go with him when he goes for walks to protect him from the dogs and kids."

"You live near here?" Asked Maktu.

"No ... " He smiled, "I live there." He made a sweeping gesture with his hand and then pointed to the top of a giant oak tree protruding above the immediate canopy.

"In one of those skyscrapers?" Maktu asked.

"Not so high... up in one of these trees." He smiled and gestured towards a particularly thick cluster of trees recessed off the main trail.

"Amazing!" Exclaimed Maktu. "A man to my liking." He grinned at the man.

"I too live far from the madding crowd... in the 'wilderness' of northern Canada. And I too have wild creatures for companions."

The man studied Maktu closely and then Christina.

"No, " She said, "he's not lying. But he cuts down the trees to make a shelter!"

For a long moment the Park man studied them. The skunk as well studied them closely and found them friendly and waddled forward and rubbed against their legs as a domestic cat might do.

"Where you from?" The man asked.

"I guess in a place called 'Lone Bull' might be as close as anywhere you might know. It is in Canada, northwestern Yukon."

The Park man didn't know Lone Bull, but he pretended he did and nodded.

"Would you like to come for tea?" The Park man offered. "I made some this morning." He grinned. "I have a Coleman stove so I can offer you hot tea. Rosebud can join us if you like".

He extended his hand. "My name is Burnaby, and this is Rosebud." They shook hands and Christina bent down and took the skunk's paw, which it lifted as a well-trained dog might.

They ducked into a low hole in the foliage which would go unnoticed if one didn't know it was there. Then they worked their way back through the undergrowth and up to the base of a giant oak. There Burnaby rummaged around in the cluster of vines and pulled on the end of a rope that fed high up into the canopy of the oak tree.

Suddenly from above a rope ladder unrolled, stopping within a couple feet of the forest floor, which he tied off on the tree's main root. He then turned and located a second rope, also looking like a vine... gave it a tug and a plastic renovated basket which in another incarnation served as soda-pop bottle case, but presently was a luxury padded nest for a skunk. Rosebud didn't stink, she masked her musk by rolling in the grass, and, as the man confessed, she had been neutered.

One side of the soda container had a side cut down halfway, and Rosebud climbed in and curled up under her tail. Burnaby pulled and she ascended to a platform high up in the cluster of oak limbs, and immediately she crawled out onto a platform.

"Sometimes, when it is cold I take her up with me, but most of the time she prefers being on the ground."

If you didn't know it was there, hidden in the vines you'd never suspect it was there, Maktu observed.

"By the way, my name is Burnaby, and this is Rosebud!" He nodded to the skunk, which was by then curled up, presumably asleep high up in the tree.

"Sometimes he gets to hanging out with the wrong crowd and comes home smelling of their perfume and I make him sleep down below.

"I'm Maktu and my life-partner Christina".

Christina's grin radiated.

"How did you and Rosebud meet?"

Burnaby smiled as he handed around drinking cups. On the bottom floor of the platform there was a flared dog dish, the kind that spreads at the bottom and impossible to tip over. .

"Some kids were throwing rocks at him here in the Park, so I started throwing rocks at them and as soon as I hit one, they quickly departed. I think one of the kids must have hit Rosebud because when he tried to run away from me, he limped badly on one leg." Burnaby gave Rosebud a pet as one might a domestic cat.

“So, I put my coat over him and took him to a sheltered place here in the forest looked him over, and sure enough one leg was skinned and swollen.

Once again, he gave the skunk a pet. “Surprisingly! He didn’t spray me, even when I wrapped him up in my coat and brought him up here. Course my clothes were a little rank for a while after that, but I don’t entertain much anyway.” He smiled.

“But, after a while he stopped being afraid of me and the situation up here, and he got to trust me. And if I did get a little rank, even by my ‘street-people’ friends’ standards, I can always just wash in the lake here in the Park.

“And you?”

“Same place... in the Park. Often, we take a joint bath, think of a parent washing a child. I sometimes use shampoo when I get to smelling worse than Rosebud.”

“You take Rosebud up the tree to keep warm?” Asked Maktu.

The man nodded.

“Which? To keep you or him warm?”

“Both. Sometimes we get sub-zero temperatures, often snow.” He paused for a moment. I do have to admit; I did have him neutered and de-skunked”.

“As I said, Burnaby, that’s my name.” he introduced himself again. pulled a fingerless glove off his right hand “I don’t have company often except Rosebud... but I think you can be trusted.”

“Maktu and Christina”. They shook hands and a paw.

“How did you come to live in Central Park?” Christina asked.

“Bored with the City I guess. You see, I was born in Hoboken, New Jersey but I was given a great pair of binoculars so I spent most of my time as a kid in the parks that had woods, just looking, studying everything I could that didn’t have a human handprint on it... trees, plants, birds and”, he nodded to Rosebud, “skunks”.

"Then one day I came across this kit-skunk that had been hurt, as I said, and by then I had made me a little fort up in the trees here in the Park so I brought him here. Skunks are omnivorous and will eat not just fruits, vegetables, and grubs, but also small mice so it was easy to find food for him.'

"I made a little fence for him but soon I took it down when he was healed. But... much to my surprise, he didn't run off."

The man stroked the skunk who rolled on its back, much like a domestic cat would to be scratched on its belly.

"This is marvellous!" Maktu exclaimed. "But what do you do in the wintertime?"

"Hoboken. If it gets really rough, I have a sister who lives there. We get along fine, but she doesn't allow pets, so Rosebud has to hibernate in the Park."

"This is lovely." Christina remarked as the tree gently rock in the canopy winds, swinging them gently as they drank their tea with the man and his pet. But finally they had to go to get ready for dinner.

"Tomorrow evening, Maktu has an art show at the Sullivan Gallery... why don't you come? Bring Rosebud. We'll tell them you're coming."

"Fantastic idea, at least we'll have a few friends there not connected to the Gallery! Do come?" Maktu invited.

"Rosebud may have to stay home." Maktu cautioned. "But if they make an issue of it, so will we!"

"I certainly can't frequent a place that doesn't let skunks in the door." Teased Christina.

"No! NO!" Snapped Maktu, "I'll tell them you're coming. If they won't let you in the doors, I'm leaving with you. " Maktu grinned, he liked the idea of having a skunk at the show, after all, his paintings are about Nature.

***

As soon as they got to their hotel, they tried on their purchases for the show the next evening.

"Oh my God!" Exclaimed Maktu as Christina came out of the dressing room. She was chic, wearing the soft-doe skin, powder-blue, thin suede dress that contoured to her body. Around her neck she wore the black obsidian neckless that made her look very Indian.

They stood side by side, looking at themselves in the mirror. "I think they'll let us in the door." Maktu smiled. "I'll tell them I am with you."

Chapter 20

Maktu arrived by cab, Marlo was there to meet him and take him up to the NBC studios. A Page took their names and guided them backstage, directly into Studio 2, the "Guest/Host Interview" studio for their early morning National News and Information" program.

Immediately he was scooped through the chaos of 'pre-live-on-air' hysteria to a burly wardrobe woman who immediately tried to force Maktu to wear a fake leather beaded jacket complete with fringe tassels.

"This will not go well", Marlo thought, and it didn't. The wardrobe attendant bristled and whined once too often, until Maktu took the fake Indian beaded, Japanese made, jacket from her and turned her with his good hand, until she could not avoid his eyes.

"Take this fake Lakota Sioux coat and stick it up your ample ass!" He glanced up and saw Marlo's eyes close. "And . . . if you have any other problems, contact my agent here." He nodded to Marlo, knowing that she would not be comprehending what had happened but sensing it had not gone well, she would contain the collateral damage.

He reached into the wardrobe rack, found a jacket that was identical to the one he'd worn when he came into the City, but not as thread bare. “If this tweed jacket is good enough for the Brooks Brothers, and Indiana Jones” who he saw in the hospital through the bandages, “it is good enough for me.”

Marlo’s sense of foreboding blossomed.

“On Set!” Someone barked from behind the lights.

“Break a leg,” Marlo whispered.

“Mine or their’s?” Maktu said, grinned and stepped before the cameras.

“This was definitely not going to be a scripted interview”, Marlo giggled quietly to herself.

Tom Branson, the usual host, has been caught on the other side of the war in Iraq and will not be doing the interviews that day, desperately in the last minute, NBC had grabbed a regional morning show host.

“Good morning, America, I’m Brad Sheldon, your host today in the absence of Tom Branson, who as many of you know is trapped in a firebase just outside of Baghdad and hasn’t been able to get out. Tom... from the people of America, we wish you a safe and spee-dee return.” He racked his cue cards and looked up into the monitor just below Camera One, he was seeing just what they were seeing including inset clips.

“To lead off today, as those of you in the art community here in New York know, there has been quite a stir in the industry over a show that will open tomorrow at the Sullivan Gallery on Park Avenue. It is the works of a Canadian artist named simply Maktu. But not just a Canadian painter, an authentic Jack London character from a very remote region in the far frozen North.

A picture taken by Chris earlier that year showing Maktu packing his snow machine with Shag sitting confidently on the back.

The host prattled on. “Mister Maktu lives in a cabin that is a full day's snowmobile run to the nearest settlement – and that the first outpost of real civilisation. And even it has a population of less than two hundred souls." The camera cut to the cover lead painting for the Gallery show, and held on it for a long moment before cutting to the host.

"We've all read Jack London and are fully aware of the perils of the North."

"Mister Maktu" the interviewer began, and the camera turned to Maktu, "I understand that it takes you a full day to go by snowmobile from your cabin on Kolsana Lake in the Yukon to the nearest settlement called Lone Bull. Is that correct?"

"True. But I understand that's no longer than walking from East Manhattan to Hoboken." Maktu replied looking at the interviewer. "And probably a whole lot safer", he added. The audience broke spontaneously into laughter before a cue card could prompt them.

The screen then showed a signature painting of a large winter forest scene with dark husks of tree trunks encircling an explosion of sunlight on fresh new snow, reminiscent of the Impressionists work. However, the camera pulled in on the painting's detail revealing closely that Maktu used an entire pallet of colours to achieve a feeling. There was an audible gasp of awe from the audience.

The producer then cut away to a few of the other paintings that Christina had sent to the Gallery and they to the television studio.

"You have been called the "Monet of the North" What do you say to that?"

"Oh shit!" Marlo swore under her breath, anticipating Maktu's response. But much to her relief, he held it together with grace.

"Oh, Monsieur Monet's French was so much better than mine!"

The audience erupted. This man was authentic, and they loved it.

Trying to bring control back to his performance as host, he said with confidence. "So, Mister Maktu ultimately, what takes you to the end of the Earth to paint? Can't you do that in a less isolated situation? .... I mean let's be truthful," the host saw the director's signal to slow down and extend the interview, which he interpreted as trying to draw out Maktu to take a free rein and layout a vision of the North, full of wolves, marauding bears, and wandering lost in endless circles... all of which the interviewer readily confessed to the audience would be his plight.

"You go out there alone, what if you chop off a toe, or a bear attacks you, or a wolf ambushes you."

There was a long pause following the man's diatribe, so long that the interviewer feared he'd have to re-ask the question.

"Well frankly, Mr. Sheldon, I'm not sure if there was a serious question there, but as for the situations you described, you'd have to be a damn fool for those events to happen." The audience lapped it up.

"But" Maktu changed the subject. "Why do I paint where I do, in what you call the 'Wilderness'?'

The interviewer nodded.

"Well, to tell you the truth," Maktu added, "it is like, I'm told, that the bank robber Willy Sutton said when asked why he robbed banks and he replied, "Because that is where the money is!"

"I paint in the 'wilderness'... as you'd call it, because it is there where the splendour, the breath-taking beauty is. It is a place that isn't of man's making. And that is where my heart resides!"

The audience was lapping it up, and the program director motioned to the Interviewer to continue and extend the interview.

"I mean, you live, as I understand it in a cabin on a lake miles and miles from your nearest neighbours. Does your cabin have any modern conveniences?"

"Like a dry roof?"

"Like indoor plumbing!" He paused for an answer that did not come.

"I mean, it must be hell, no TV, no internet, not even indoor running water. Let me ask you, do you have an outhouse?

"Of course!"

"Why?"

"Why?!" Maktu repeated astonished. He thought for a moment, "Well, for sanitation convenience, and aesthetics of course, and with an indoor toilet you miss so much!" He paused.

"An outhouse, on the other hand, does take a lot more effort, but often it can be a 'once in a lifetime' experience!" "I bet." The host said under his breath, thinking about the raw cold and a lone figure trudging through a deep snow-banked trail to a lone unlit building.

As though reading the host's thoughts Maktu replied. "Why not indoor plumbing, you ask?"

"Outside, if you look up instead of down at your feet," he said. "You look up at the stars fresh, vivid, unfiltered by ambient lights. Quite often you'll catch a meteor-shower so charged that it seems like giants are throwing balls of fire across the sky."

He looked out to the audience as though talking directly to them "And often the Northern Lights are so strong you can find every colour in the rainbow snake-dancing across the sky.... and, so they are vivid, you can actually hear them!"

Maktu's enthusiasm had caught the imagination of the audience, the camera crew, even the jaded producer.

"And... It sounds like Velcro being ripped apart." It was a

sound all knew.

"Sure, you pay the dues of having to put on a parka and snow-boots, gloves, etc. but the benefit of the experience far surpasses the hassles. In the North you do what you have to, but the rewards are humbling!" He smiled to the audience, and they smiled back.

The next question on the host's list was "What are you running away from... out there in the wilderness!

For Maktu, it was a ridiculous question.

"I am not running away from anything... I'm running to something. Something so spectacular that any 'hardships' as you infer, are but a small price to pay for the rewards." He sat silently for a moment.

"If you knew the experience, you'd know it is a ridiculous question!"

Sensing that the interviewer himself had never been in the 'wilderness' as he called it... nor for that matter had seen Maktu's paintings first hand, nor even had any interest in his art, Maktu rose from his chair, smiled at the camera, turned to the audience gave them a big embracing smile, bowed, removed his microphone, smiled yet again and walked off camera!

There was a long moment of shocked silence... and then a loud impromptu explosion of applause!

Quickly the program host jumped in, "Thank you Mr. Maktu!" He looked desperately at his notes.

"Saturday Evening, Sullivan Gallery for Fine Art... Doors open at 7:00 PM."

Marlo, standing off stage, was wiping tears from her eyes, the consequence of laughing.

"Well, that went rather well!" She took his hand and started quickly for the stage door.

Chapter 21

Brandon took Maktu and Christina to the '21 Club' before the Gallery's opening. Maktu was too nervous to eat hors d'oeuvres, or even sit down, and Jack Kriendler, one of the two owner-brothers took him for a tour of their collection of cowboy oriented Western Art. Kriendler pointed out that many of the artists had much in common with their subjects. Charles Russel and Fredrick Remington were cowboys themselves. Maktu was so fascinated by their art that he soon forgot that he himself was to be the subject of a showing of his work in one of New York's most prestigious galleries.

"Don't be afraid." his Grandmother used to council him on the rare occasions when they did go into to town for supplies. "We all come from the same place and we're all going back to the same place!"

She never elaborated where that 'same place' was, nor what it looked like when she consoled him about going to town for supplies. Nor did she elaborate about what to do when they'd intercept 'town boys' that might tease him about his clothes or shy manner. Her council when he associated with other boys was "they all put on their pants one leg at a time, just like you!"

He never quite understood what it meant, but he did realise at family gatherings, that the other kids were envious of him living in what they called, the "wilderness".

Brandon looked at his watch when the tour of the '21 Club's art collection was finished.

"Time to see if my gamble on your talent is correct." Brandon pushed himself back from the table with a grin that said he already knew the results of his 'gamble".

Marlo opened the doors to the Gallery at exactly 7:00... And soon the place was packed– initially with the curious to see what would induce Brandon to take such a chance on an unknown artist from the "Wilderness" of Canada. But soon the Gallery became infiltrated with serious art collectors.

Marlo was brilliant as she guided the Artist through the gallery audience, singling out the patrons and the serious collectors, giving each requisite access to Maktu but still moving them though the entire collection. Once the serious collectors had done the tour and were focused on a particular piece, they would be introduced to Maktu, and then if their interest was serious, into Brandon's office. And, if there was a serious sale pending, the doors of the office would be closed until there was a decision before being reopened. If there was a sale, Brandon would nod to Marlo who would go the painting in question and put a small gold star sticker on its identification card. If the sale was pending under further consideration, it would be a purple star.

Also, Marlo's instincts were impeccable in determining the serious patrons from the wanna-bes as she guided them through the collection.

"I know something about Art," said a bombastic viewer anxious to make as much an impression on Maktu as his paintings did on the man. "And I see a lot of Cézanne in your paintings." He said full of self-inflated importance.

"Oh," confessed Maktu, "I doubt that. I've never met the

man!"

Midway through the evening, as Maktu was visiting with no less than the Mayor of the City, he heard a commotion behind him and there was Christina grinning and holding 'Rosebud' the skunk!

Suddenly the Art and Artist became secondary to the surrounding audience who either retreated or crowded to pet the skunk.

"Is Burnaby here?" He asked, taking the skunk in his arms and giving her a nose-to-nose rub. The media loved the photo op.

"Right behind you." The man from the Park laughed. The media in attendance loved the photo-shoot opportunity and the marketing hook of a wild animal from City Park attending an art show of a man the 'Wilderness' was perfect!

"It is time." Said Brandon to Maktu. "Time for the Artist to talk about his work!" The idea staggered Maktu, but Christina took his good hand. (He still wore the customised glove to accommodate the missing fingers, and the special dark mountaineering glasses to adjust the light to his eyes).

The Gallery owner turned to Maktu. "You're the main attraction tonight! If the show's attendants want to look at skunks, I suggest they go to the zoo!" He tried to look stern, but he grinned and gave Rosebud a pet.

Before Maktu gave the skunk back, the media snapped a series of shots of the artist holding Rosebud in front of the show's signature painting of a rugged mountain peak at sunrise in pastel, early dawn colours.

"May I have your attention." Brandon spoke loudly in the main rotunda of the Gallery. He too stood in front of the show's signature painting, a large four foot by five-foot canvas of a snow-capped mountain peak caught in a brilliant at sunrise. It was the painting used for the invitations and the Gallery handout brochure.

“As many of you know, my family has hosted in our gallery many world-famous artists, but never one of such natural talent as the man who it is my pleasure to introduce tonight. ”

“But first, I ’d like to give you a little profile of this man’s background because it will serve to enhance your understanding of his natural talent.”

He turned and looked at Maktu, who looked down humbly at his feet. “Maktu is an Indigenous Tlingit Native man from a very remote region of the Yukon in Northwestern Canada”.

“He lives on a remote lake accessible in the winter only by a snowmobile, or snowshoes, or a dogsled and in emergencies by floatplane and in the summer by either a boat with an outboard motor, or a canoe”.

“I first saw Maktu’s work in the Yukon when I was there fly-fishing for cut-throat trout. I was so captivated by the brilliance in what I saw that I went to some effort to find out who he was”.

“What I discovered is a rare, raw talent sequestered in what we might call a “true wilderness”, but one that Maktu calls ‘home”.

“I can go on about this man’s talents and his authenticity but, I have asked instead for Maktu, himself to speak.

Maktu took a deep breath. “I am humbled to be here. I have never been in a room with so many important people in my life... at least not one where there wasn’t a hockey puck and hockey sticks involved.”

The laughter broke the ice and gave Maktu confidence to continue. He smiled.

“Who motivated you to paint?” Asked a journalist from the Village Voice.

Maktu spoke without hesitation. “My Grandmother.” He paused and organised his thoughts. Her memory gave him courage to continue.

“I was orphaned at a young age and was raised by my grandparents in a very remote Indian Village called K’ewanka and later in the larger village of K’weset, both located in the Territory you call the Yukon.”

“My Gran loved to paint and when we went out to Whitehorse... which was only twice a year, to trade the furs my Grandfather trapped over the Winter, she would buy food staples, and if there was money left over, also paints and canvases, but...” He looks a little sheepishly “generally we scrounged for art material”s.

“Is it true that your first paintings were with leftover house paints from the dump, and worn-out tent canvas?’ Asked a journalist.

A flash of anger sparked in Maktu, thinking he was being ridiculed, and he glanced at Brandon who read his look and shook his head for Maktu not to react as though he were being put down.

“Well sure, most of the money went for necessities like canned goods, flour, cooking oil, etcetera. And yes, often we got old tent canvases and paints came from near-empty house-paint cans from the dump.”

He chuckled, “Maybe that is why my early paintings were all in pastels... thinking back about the pastel suburbs of Whitehorse.” He thought about the idea for a moment and nodded confirming it to himself. “Ya... probably.” He smiled. Brandon smiled at Marlo and gave her a thumbs up.

“Did she teach you how to draw?” asked another reporter.

“No, not at all. She taught me that subject has three elements, the subject and it’s colour, even if it is just black and white, and the third...” he paused, unsure... “the ‘feeling’ of the subject.” He fell silent for a moment. “I guess I think mainly about capturing the ‘feeling’! If you want exactness of detail, use a camera.”

"What advice would you give artist today?" Asked Cowboy Bob reading from a note scribbled on a piece of paper and passed to him by his Uncle Brandon.

"I would say just what my Grandmother said to me. Paint not just what you see, but what you feel about the subject, and if you capture it, you will never see the subject without thinking about it".

He glanced at Christina who gave him a thumbs-up and a radiant smile.

It was a perfect point to terminate the Interview. "Don't paint just what you see... but also what feel! A camera can capture whet you see. But for me, I paint what I feel!" He smiled and his eyes engaged the cameras and the viewing audience.

"Gunaicheesh." He said.

"What does that mean?"

Maktu's smile radiated. He took Christina's hand and gave it a squeeze then smiled to the gathering.

"Thank you... in Tlingit" He released Christina and reached out to Marlo who still held Rosebud, took from her the skunk and cradled it in his arms. Because the interview was conducted in front of the "Mountain at Sunrise" painting, with the artist rubbing noses with the skunk, it was used in all the dailies and on the New York based television stations that covered the show.

"Paint what you feel not just what you see!" Were his closing words.

Then, suddenly another idea came to him. "AND ...I think there is no subject more spectacular than this City at night!" He smiled to the audiences both in the gallery and those viewing the television his audience.

Again, he said "Gunaicheesh. Thank you" he repeated, grinned, shook one more hand. It was the Mayor's.

Though the show's launch lasted but a few hours, both Brandon and Marlo were ecstatic with how it went. Cowboy Bob interceded and suggested he take Maktu and Christina for a night in New York ... "Tour of the Town", starting in Harlem and a night club that featured a black woman blues singer. Christina knew of the Club in Harlem and confirmed that it was a great idea.

Maktu had had no interaction with the black culture and was enthralled with both the scene and the performer's performance. Between sets, she joined them at their table and immediately she was as interested in meeting a real Indian as he was of meeting her. And likely they would have remained there until closing time, but Cowboy Bob had an agenda, and his next stop was further Upton at a Brazilian club where they specialised in "Soca" music.

It was around 22nd Avenue that Maktu, feeling the effects of the atmosphere he'd had in Harlem, asked Cowboy Bob "how fast will your car go?"

The streets were empty at that time of night.

"I don't know... let's see!" and between and 22nd Avenue and 23rd, he jammed the gas pedal to the floor!

The first police car wasn't until 25th Avenue, and then it was far back. But by 28th there was a second one and gaining.

Cowboy Bob called out the speedometer readings... "75 miles per hour, 8o and finally 87 when he realised that they were being chased and the police had an advantage, of a police call radio. They hoped that no one was coming across the streets on the perpendicular.

"Is this as fast as she'll go?" Asked Maktu loving the adventure.

"Hang on!". Their gain in speed was noticeable... but they now had another police car joining in the pursuit, but he was still blocks away.

"Ready? At the next alley I'm going to turn off my lights and cut down it!... So hang on!!"

Double clutching down the gears and using the hand brake until the smoking break-drum burned their eyes, then cranking the steering wheel hard to the right, they shot down the alley. Finding a dumpster, Bob cut in behind it and turned off the car lights and engine.

They sat there frozen as the first pursuing police car shot past, and then the second.

Hunkered in behind the trash dumpster they laughed hysterically and rolled out of the car.

Maktu looked up. Sandwiched between the skyscrapers was the moon... slightly waning, but mostly full!!

"What a wonderful ending," Maktu laughed, "to a great experience that started at my cabin a world away –and now to hiding out in New York City from the Law, after a great gallery show.

Suddenly he was blinded by a high-beam spotlight. His first response was to grab Christina and make a run for it down the alley in the other direction, but just then another police car closed off that route.

Realising they were trapped, Maktu whispered. "We'll tell them I was driving!"

"It is my fault, officers. I am not from here, and I wanted to learn how to drive in the City, but the only time I can practice in this City is at night!" Maktu doubted they'd believe him, but it helped take the heat off Bob.

"You see I've never gone any faster than a snowmobile or a dog team." He added for authenticity and actually it was the truth!

*****

"What are the charges?" The woman Judge asked.

"Reckless driving. Driving without a legal driver's license."

"What do you have to say to these charges? How do you plead Mister Maktu?"

Suddenly the reality of a criminal charge in a foreign country came upon him and he became very conciliatory. "Your honour. I came to New York City to attend an opening of an art show of my work."

He paused. "But, your Honour, I don't know what came over me. I've never been arrested... in fact I'm not even from here. I'm from Canada!"

"And that is your defence?" The judge, a woman, who, gauging by her wire-rim glasses over which she looked at him; she was a no-nonsense Judge, and particularly at 2:00 AM.!

"Wait, I know you... you're the artist who terminated the interview with that stand-in host on NBC this morning!" She studied him confirming her observation.

"Yes, I do know you." She said without expression. "I thought you handled yourself very well, and that jerk interviewer deserved your response."

She smiled. "Still the charges against you are very serious. Reckless Driving at speeds in excess of eighty miles per hour. No valid driver's license."

Maktu realised that he had never had a driver's license, even a Canadian one, and he wondered if soon would be a good time the get one.

The Judge looked hard at him. But there was a twinkle in her eyes. "Since you are not from here and therefore not familiar with our traffic laws, I here-by fine you 'Court Costs' and a warning not to drive again while you are here until you get a license."

Then she smiled. "By the way, that host needed some trimming!" She looked at him and smiled and then at the Bailiff.

"Next case!" He called out.

Chapter 22

It was after 8:00 a.m. when Maktu heard a slight sound outside his door. Cautiously he eased out of bed and quietly opened the door and there on the floor-mat was a fat Weekend edition of the New York Times. Quietly he bent down and brought it in and laid it on the coffee table. He opened the curtains upon the City. Without, the tapestry of City-lights and traffic, it was quiet, and the air seemed like a fresh flower garden in bloom. Did anyone live there behind those windows? Maktu wondered. He gazed out of the window, enthralled that tens of thousands of people lived and worked there during the week behind all the windowed towers, but now the city seemed empty.

He eased over to the phone and pushed the 'Desk' button, then whispered an order for two coffees and some fresh pastries.

"It will be right up." The desk clerk said. And ten minutes later there came a quiet knock at the door.

Gently he gave Christina a light shake and kissed her forehead. "It is time to face yet another day in "Tower Town"... a name he'd coined.

She rolled over, smiled, looked out at the City's profile, smiled again and took his hand. "I love you!" She whispered.

"Be careful what you say, your words could have repercussions."

She rose, picked up a Hotel robe and went into the bathroom. Maktu heard the shower and soon she came out wrapped in a thick Park Lane robe.

"Coffee?"

Purposefully, Maktu insisted on pouring, then handing Christina the Times

Immediately she rustled through it until she found the 'Sunday Section', pulled it out and rifled through the Sections until she came to the column by Mrs. Walton. She looked up at Maktu questioningly?

"Well, it could be worse." He grinned.

The column began: *As many know I have been doing this weekly Art Column for almost twenty years. And as many will attest, I have covered art in many forms from Warhol to the Wyeths, and I must confess I've become a little jaded. So, when Brandon Sullivan asked me to come by the Sullivan Gallery and look at his newest show, I expected another 'same old', but I accepted out of respect for Brandon's judgement.*

Brandon was cagey and insisted that I see the show that they'd just set up first before meeting the artist or even knowing anything about him or even the subject. They had just finished hanging it before the interview and I would be the first person to see this artist's work from the Yukon in Canada.

To summarise the show in a word... "Breath-taking!"

The subject of this one-person show is the 'Northern Canadian Wilderness', and it is the "wilderness" that very few people have ever experienced! In fact, the show has rightly been called, "In the Absence of Man" for it is the consequence of a person who lives deeply sequestered in a land where few humans have ever ventured! On a map, it is the vast Canadian mountains West of Whitehorse to the Pacific.

His subject is not the view that a visitor might see. It is without

hyperbole ...a land where man is an 'oddity'.

Without any formal training in art except from his Grandmother, and using left over house paints on cardboard, Maktu started a journey that would one day land him with a show in one of New York's most prestigious galleries.

"I've had no real lessons." He apologetically admits. "In fact, I don't really paint what most people see. Rather, it is what I feel! For me, Nature is a changing tapestry that goes beyond our observations. My 'Gran' used to counsel me to look beyond the limits of the eye to the feelings that a subject or a scene produces".

"A tree has a predictable shape, but the ever-changing light challenges me to dissect it into the parts. When a logger sees a tree, he sees it as wood, squared beams, boards. When I see a tree, I see how it reflects light into essences."

To illustrate his point, Maktu pointed to a small 8"x10" painting of a pinecone covered with frozen frost to illustrates his point. From afar it is a pinecone, but drawn into its unity, it is a complex of a pointillist's palate of colours in every shade.

"Snow is not white!" Said Maktu. "It radiates every colour in the rainbow! You, just have to train your eye to see it... to dissect it into its components." "And" he adds. "Once seen, it can never be unseen."

"Once this show has been seen," she wrote, "the Natural subject can never be unseen! And. it does enhances one's perspective...forever."

She concluded, keeping her column short so there was room for pictures of two of his paintings. Something she had never done!

Before closing the interview, I asked the hanging question, "Don't you get lonely out there by yourself". "Of course, you can only tell yourself the same joke so many times." He laughed.

"Is that because you've never met a partner who loves the wilderness as much as you?"

"No ... in fact, I have met her... but I am not a courageous man and I'm afraid to ask!" He replied.

"Well..." I said to him, "If she reads this column–you just did!'

"Sullivan Gallery for Fine Art. It is certainly worth a visit!"

"Yes!" Christina screamed so loud that Rosebud in the Park could have heard her! "YES! I will be your bride and partner for the rest of our lives!" She dropped the paper and threw her arms around him.

Grinning, he handed her the ring box from Tiffany's.

Cautiously she opened it ... BUT! instead of a jewelled ring there was a cigar band in the slot where a ring should be.

"It is a 'placeholder' until we can go there, and you can choose one that you like." He grinned, "Choose well, you will be wearing it for the rest of your life! After all it is your chance to live the life, you said you'd like to live!"

"NICE," She said quietly. "I accept!"

"We will have to stay one more day so you can choose well at Tiffany's... after all you will be wearing it for a long time!"

After coffee and breakfast pastries, the phone rang.

Though Maktu was the closest to the phone he was terrified to answer it. He had only on very rare occasions spoken into a non-radiophone, one where there was only one person on the line instead of a multitude of 'bush' inhabitants.

It was Brandon. "We just read Mrs Walton's column in the Times. Congratulations!" He exclaimed.

When he heard that Maktu and Christina were staying an extra day, he spoke with his wife then immediately called to invite them to supper at their home in "Upper Manhattan.". which, Maktu wondered if the name applied not for the location but to the altitude.

"Just push the top floor button. It will read 'Penthouse'. Maktu ran the invitation pass Christina, she smiled and nodded still in a state of shock from being proposed to in front of all of the New York Times reading audience.

"But tell him we can't come until sunset; we have a previous engagement".

Curious, since all Brandon knew of their plans had been to return to Canada early the next at evening but had suddenly changed them.

"Anyone I know?" He asked.

"Probably not!" said Maktu.

"I know a lot of people in New York. What is their name? Maybe they could join us."

"Rosebud."

"Oh God!" He exclaimed under his breath. With a name like that, she has to be a con-artist or a 'hooker' and suddenly he felt responsible for the couple. Though he obviously knew Maktu was from the far reaches of the Yukon wideness and might be vulnerable to seduction into some scam. Christina had gone to a prestigious girl's school in Bryn Mawr, where Lincoln Continentals and Porsches were used to pick up kids from schools and run to the store for groceries. He even had two steady clients from there, certainly Christina would be aware of someone named 'Rosebud'.

"Would I know her?" He asked, trying not to sound protective.

"Not unless you hang around Central Park... she's a Skunk!"

"The one from the show last night? I'm sorry," he apologised once he stopped laughing. "but we are not having skunk food for supper."

"Oh, that's alright, she will have had supper. In fact, I don't think she's normally allowed out after sunset. Last night was an exception".

Still laughing, he repeated his address and what time to come.

*****

"How did the rest of the show go?" came a voice from behind them as Maktu and Christina strolled through Central Park. It was Burnaby. "We had to leave early – Rosebud's bedtime."

As usual the man and his skunk were pursued by a crowd of squealing little kids admiring Rosebud, feeding her with peanuts, sometimes handheld, sometimes hand thrown.

Burnaby could see the skunk was no longer enjoying the adoration when Rosebud turned to Burnaby and looked for help.

Immediately Burnaby turned and told the kids to go home ... but if that was ineffective, all Rosebud had to do was to lift her tail. She never had to spray for no sooner did she make the tail gesture, then the admirers became frightened by stories about the strength and capacity of a skunk's spray and were immediately gone.

"So, how did it go?" Burnaby asked again. "Rosebud was getting cranky from all of the attention."

"Honestly, I don't know. To tell you the truth, I don't know much of anything about the show... I was in a state of shock! ... I'm not even sure if we sold a single painting".

"You really are a wonderful artist. Your winter paintings made me want to go to northern Canada!"

"How were sales?"

"I have no idea, but no one threw eggs, and the police didn't get called."

Burnaby looked at Christina.

She smiled. "I don't know either, but I had a wonderful time! I'd sent out an invitation to all of my school friends, which was easy since most of them live within a few blocks of each other, in Pennsylvania, just outside of New York."

She smiled and confessed, "When I went North to the 'Wilds' of the Canadian North, they all told me that I was crazy! But, when they met Maktu and saw how talented he is, and how spectacular the country is, I think they were all a little jealous of how things worked out for me." She smiled.

"So... tell us what you think?" She asked Burnaby once they got to the tree platform and Burnaby lit the Coleman for tea.

"Rosebud and I had a marvellous time! Even met the Mayor! I didn't tell him we were living in his Park, for free!" Burnaby laughed.

They soon fell silent enjoying each other's company and the tree swaying gently as they drank their tea, Rosebud curled up in Christina's lap and fell asleep.

"No man, you really are a great artist!" Said Burnaby as they said their good-byes at the base of the tree.

It was after dark when the couple said goodbye to Burnaby and his pet, and went back to the hotel to change, then took a taxi to the address Brandon gave them. It also was on the Park, though the taxi charged them anyway.

"Buddy, this is a dog-eat-dog world, get used to it!"

Still Maktu gave him a tip about planting his crops early!

Following Brandon's instructions to his suite, Maktu's ears popped from the rapid ascent in altitude change going up to the top floor of the Manhattan skyscraper. Then, when the door opened it was directly into the private foyer on the top floor penthouse.

"Welcome!" Brandon greeted them as the doors opened. A lady in a casual evening dress came forward from a side hall.

"May I introduce my wife and life-partner." Maktu, Christina, this is Sarah, many years my partner.... Twenty-seven in fact! "

The woman who stepped around him from behind was dressed in a comfortable, though obviously not cheap cocktail dress. She smiled and graciously extended her hand.

"Sarah." She smiled.

"I attended your show last night." she said after the introductions. "You are just as Brandon claimed, a "great artist" and, just as Brandon also claims, you're definitely not pretentious or arrogant about it." She smiled.

"In fact, he said he had to go all the way to the far reaches of Canada to find you."

"Well not exactly, but it makes for a good story." Maktu laughed.

Maktu was always nervous about meeting white people, especially if they were from outside the Valley... certainly never ones who lived in a building that stretched up into the clouds.

"Chris, a pilot friend, used to say about social occasions with White people. "When in doubt, 'Smile'."

Sarah turned to Christina, "and you are as just as striking as Marlo and Brandon claimed."

"And you can add," Brandon nodded at his wife, "that I have an excellent taste in women."

"Agreed." Sarah said jokingly, then wrinkled her nose, for she detected a very faint smell which she recognised as skunk.

"Skunks!" She said with some disdain. "They've taken over the City!" She growled.

"Wouldn't that be lovely." Responded Maktu.

"Later." Brandon whispered to his wife. "I'll explain later."

"Come." He turned and led them into the penthouse's living room.

A butler appeared and extended his arms for their coats.

Maktu drew back, not understanding that he would, in fact, get the coat back at the end of the evening.

"OH MY!" Maktu gasped as they entered the living room. Just as their Hotel room had a commanding view over Central Park, Brandon's and Sarah's was a spectacular view of the entire city, from above!

"Excuse me," the butler interjected. "What will you be having to drink?"

"Spring water." Maktu responded. Christina gave his hand a squeeze.

"In sorry." Said Brandon to the butler, "We are all having Dom Perrier."

Maktu wrinkled his face not understanding what Dom Perrier was. After his family's death, he never drank alcohol.

Assuming it was a type of Manhattan bottled water, Maktu nodded. Sarah, Brandon and Christina smiled at each other.

The apartment was gorgeous, even to Christina, who was accustomed to the top of the City's skyline.

The living room encompassed a wide horizon that swept a hundred degree or better of skyline view.

"Maktu" Brandon broke the painter's trance. "Tell me more about something you told me when we first began communicating. You said that you were born in the 'wilderness' and raised there by your Grandparents because your immediate family, your parents and an older brother and sister were killed in a car accident.... and that you spoke only Tlingit in your teens and when they died and you were a very young and then raised in a small Indian village in the wilderness. Where did you learn so much about the white culture?"

"Over the years it has been through my friend Chris, he is what you call a 'bush pilot'. I've never made many friends, Native or non-native. But Chris has kind of taken me under his 'wing... so to speak." He laughed at the pun, "I've learned to read English through Chris's help, in fact, he started bringing me "Dick and Jane" books and now I'm reading crime novels. In fact, he came down with plates and utensils once and taught me how to eat at White people's tables."

Maktu fell silent for a conspicuous moment. "In fact, the paints and canvases I used for this year's 'collection', as you call it, came from Chris." Maktu smiled, thinking. "I'll have to pay him back as soon as we get home." His voice had a strange detachment to it.

"Where is he?" Asked Brandon. "Where does he reside?"

Christina caught Brandon's eye and gave an imperceptible look that said to change the conversation's direction. "Do you ever get tired of this view?" She interjected. Brandon realised for reasons unknown, to drop the subject of Chris.

Speaking directly to Maktu. Mrs. Sullivan interrupted. "Excuse me, I tried to think of what you would like that you're not accustomed to for supper, and what we have decided to do is cook up a few samples of some international dishes common here in New York but maybe not in ... where is it? Lone Bull?"

"So, we are having Italian. French, Spanish German, Ukrainian and an American apple pie for dessert. Is that alright?"

"Oh my God!" Exclaimed Maktu. "When you come to Canada I can only make for you Tlingit food! Indian salmon for colour, meat is Caribou, moose, or deer".

"Oh, we have Indian restaurants." Sarah replied.

"I was talking about real 'Indians', as in Tlingit Indians." He smiled. “As in Indians and Cowboys.” They all laughed.

“This is wonderful,” Christina smiled as she recognised the taste of the first dish, “*syrniki*” a white Ukrainian pastry. As a child, Christina’s Grandmother made it, a soft white cheese similar to cottage cheese.

“Oh my gosh!” said Brandon remarked. “My family, two generations back, were from Kyiv. My great grandfather swan the Dnieper River to escape the influence of the Russian Revolution in 1917.”

Christina broke out laughing. “So did mine! My original last name was Prahojnuck!”

“And Branowich ” I say that with pride, my family is third generation removed from Kyiv.”

“Oh my!” Said Brandon. “We may be related! Certainly, taste in artists.”

They all laughed, all feeling very comfortable in the other’s company.

“So, what is new in Lone Bull?” Brandon asked over supper.

Maktu told them about about McLeod willing his mine to the people of the Valley and the formation of a Company that would soon be issuing shares in it for actual trading.

“Maybe we should buy some in case the New York stock market crashes ... again!”. Sarah laughed.

“Not a bad idea,” remarked Brandon – only half joking.

After supper they moved from the dining room table to a large crescent shaped couch out in the living room facing 270 degrees out over the City.

Maktu opted to stand to stretch his back which, if he sat too long, still spiked with stabs of pain from the snowmobile collision with a slab of shore-ice.

“Oh my God!” Maktu exclaimed suddenly. “We’re

neighbours! I can see the top of our Hotel!" He laughed. "In fact, I can see our room!" He smiled pointing out into the vast lake of lights. "I told you to close the curtains, our neighbours could be watching".

"Well, except for a few blocks over and hundreds of feet below!" Brandon grinned. "that is the case! It is the vertical drop that wears you out!" Brandon laughed, then stood and turned to Maktu and Christina.

"Come, there is something I want to show you that I *share only with very few people!"*

The couple followed Brandon into the art dealer's office.

Unlike the Sullivan Gallery the walls were all glass, all but one wall and that one had only a single painting on it.

Brandon waited until they were in the room and closed the door to shut out the ambient light of the living room and floor to ceiling curtains shutting out the light of the city. He positioned them facing a dark wall and got them to stand where the artist would stand painting it.

He turned up the lights centred directly on just the piece of art.

Illuminated by the single light it was a woman sitting in front of a fireplace in a chair, holding a baby and staring into the blazing fireplace.

Maktu had never seen a painting so magnificent, so captivating in its artistry. From the power of this simple scene, for the first time in years, tears welled in his eyes for it reminded him vividly of his own mother holding his younger brother, looking into the fire, absorbed by worry, when his father was away alone on the trap-line. Away on those bitter cold sub-subzero nights where sometimes, the only the sound punctuating the winter night, was of trees rupturing lengthways with a rifle report, and inside the sparks from the fire.

Brandon studied his guests faces. He could tell that Maktu got the message. "Exactly!" He said to Maktu. "You got the message. It is not how an image is expressed, it is not the technique, it is the mood, capturing the fullness of the moment".

"Your paintings are not just pictures; they convey moods and feelings for the subject. Your colours, your brush strokes go beyond the physical subject... they express the feelings of the moment, the "moods" of it".

As Maktu stared at the painting in disbelief of its power, he realised it was not just the subject that held its energy, it was the handling of the paint that commanded its power... the actual strokes, their fiery boldness juxtaposed against soft silence. Yes, it was the 'feeling' of it that gave it, its command.

For Maktu, it was a life altering moment for suddenly he saw it all through a different lens.

He approached the painting and studied the handling of the paint, the actual strokes that made it so powerful. He had, though his exposure was limited, never seen a painting so powerful. The fire and its reflection were dramatic in their influence! But there was something else. It was the mood.. that captured the essence of the moment.

His eyes drifted to the bottom of the painting and its very ornate frame, too small to read from afar. He approached the a brass plaque with an inscription written upon it.

"Oh my God! " Maktu gasped, then looked at the painting again and then at Brandon, for confirmation. Brandon smiled and nodded "I certainly hope so!"

"Man At Sea"

Vincent Van Gogh

"My father acquired it during the great depression." Brandon said, then laughed, "Maybe someday your paintings will command as much respect because you too have a gift for capturing the power of the moment..."

"No..." He stopped and thought, "No, the very mood ... the very essence!" "And ... you don't have to go insane to do it!"

Brandon looked at both of them and gave his ear a slight tug. "Mums the word!" I can own this and share it with special people who would admire it safely if no one knows what or where it is. I share it with very few people.

"But!" Christina nodded at Maktu. "I'd like him to keep his ears if possible?" She smiled.

There came a tap on the study door. Sarah was holding a phone. "There is a call for Maktu! It's Marlo." She gave the receiver to Maktu.

Puzzled, he took the phone looking at Sarah questioningly.

"Hello? This is Maktu." There followed a long silence from him as Marlo spoke to him, and him alone. ... and then he gasped! "Well, shewwa shewwa" he exclaimed!

"What does that mean?"

"Mighty good! Might good!!"

"Oh Marlo... true??!" His voice faltered. "Really?!!"

Again, He listened. "Oh my God! Does Brandon know?" His eyes shot to his host with disbelief! "I'll be God Damned! And Brandon hasn't said anything all night?!"

Brandon grinned. Maktu looked in Christina's eyes. "The show has sold out! Every one of the lot either has an outright sold sticker or a 'Hold 'for pick-up".

He looked at her, not fully convinced..."SOLD OUT!" He repeated

When the evening ended, Brandon walked the couple to the elevator and opened the apartment door for Maktu and Christina to leave. The night had gone far better than he had hoped!

At the door Brandon extended his hand. "And just think, if it weren't for your dog, those paintings might still be on the bottom of a remote Canadian lake!"

"And," Christina interjected, "if it were it not for our dog, the Artist would be there with them!"

Chapter 23

.

Even with two backhoes working steadily on the road over the mountain pass connecting the Lone Bull Valley with the rest of the Yukon to the East, working six days a week; the Valley was still sealed off from the outside except for the airstrip. Though there was one backhoe machine coming from each side of the divide, their progress was tediously slow due to the ferocity of the avalanches and that the snow had been compacted to concrete.

Smooth Fenton, the machine operator from the Lone Bull side, had been three weeks digging at the hard snowpack blocking the road from Whitehorse. Slowly advancing up the mountain he had never experienced snow of such density and he wondered what could trigger such an avalanche.

Suddenly, early in the 11th day, near the top of the Divide, he was momentarily blinded by a flash of brilliant silver light! It came from above, from an alpine pass well above timberline between two twin peaks of raw rock.

He wasn't even sure until he shifted his head slightly causing the light to disappear that he actually saw something. But, when he looked back, it reappeared, reassuring him it was not his imagination.

Turning off his machine, he radioed the other backhoe

operator on the other side of the pass that he was taking a break to go investigate something and untying his snowshoes from outside cabin of the machine, he started up towards the light.

It was only when he got close to the snow drifting through the mountain divide that he realised what was the source of the reflection ... it was a side mirror from an aircraft. And, judging by the fragments of the craft scattered across the snow and exposing pieces of the metal sections of the fuselage, there had been an explosion with sections of the shattered machine scattered over a vast area.

Suddenly it all made sense. The pilot was probably Chris, and he must have taken off from the Lone Bull airstrip, circled out over the Lake for altitude and turned to the West, possibly assuming he could fly through the mountain pass between the two peaks – in the clouds!

As Smooth approached the crash site of the helicopter, or what was left of it, his heart stopped! Then he saw, up close, a section of the main rotor-blade bent at a violent arthritic angle, and wedged into a boulder pile thirty meters away! He immediately recognised it by the stripes on the blade... it was definitely off Chris's helicopter!

Digging back though the snow at the exposed blackened rock wall, he realised that there must have been an explosion of such magnitude and violence, that it likely triggered the chain of avalanches that ran all around the Lake. The cornices, already loaded with a hard winter's snow-load, and pregnant with weight from a warm early Spring, the explosion of the crash triggered the avalanches encircling the Pass, and they in turn the next until the shock-waves unleashed a deadly concert of violent avalanches for fifty kilometres of shock-waves each more powerful than the last, triggering the cornices on the adjacent peaks, and each pregnant snowpack pack gave birth at the slightest provocation. The explosion of a helicopter would have been equal to many sticks of dynamite to run the full length of the lake.

Suddenly it all made sense. Chris must had lifted off from the airport's landing pad with the first light, but the mountain pass that was a short-cut to Maktu's was still socked in with early morning fog. But he knew as Chris used to say, he knew every rock marmot that lived on the vertical walls intimately. He was accustomed to flying through it having after a long history of doing it many times on rescue missions. He must have assumed he could do it blindly since he knew it so well. And possibly for the personal thrill, when he was alone, he'd go into a blind mountain-pass with just a few feet between rock walls, based on a brief glance.

Smooth climbed to where the cockpit should be, but there was only a huge blacken imprint on a sheer granite wall, after the explosion there was nothing left, certainly nothing of Chris's remains. Ironically, one rotor-blade lay intact fifty yards from the wreckage, but that was all that remained.

Smooth radioed down to Chance's sideband radio at the Store. In turn, Chance relayed the findings to the Search and Rescue station in Whitehorse. With the road still not completely opened from neither the East nor West, Search and Rescue sent a forensic team by helicopter to retrieve what information could be gleamed from the crash.

By mid-afternoon, a forensic team helicoptered over from Whitehorse and radioed back confirming what Smooth had surmised from the stripes on the rotor blade and the tail sections of the helicopter that it was Chris's machine and the explosion was of such magnitude that it triggered the concert of avalanching cornices that reached all the way to the furtherest shoreline of the Lake.

They too concluded there was no indication of the body.

Chapter 24

"I think this Lone Bull Stock thing that the Town Council has been cooking up is a good thing for you and me," said Crank Fenton. But with the ground still frozen, it could take a few more months before we can start mining."

"So, the way I reckon, we ain't got any out of our wallets investments if we can do something to speed-up the burial process." Reasoned Smooth

"What if we ploughed the snow off a grave site and accelerated the thawing process. The way I see it, the faster the shares are transferred over to us holders, the faster we can make our fortune plans and blow this iceberg for Florida."

Crank liked things which according to his brother, were good for him and he nodded in agreement.

"You see, we all are gonna get an equal share including the Indians. And, after we get McLeod planted nice and proper, we can get started re-opening that mine of his. Some figure he may have hit that same vein all the other companies have been chasing." He rubbed his hands, pleased with his brilliance.

It had been at the wake dance by the vocal intensity of the crowd that McLeod should be kept in the town's meat house in a respectful manner since he had been detached from the chunk of spruce trunk that he'd wrapped himself around in his dying minutes, then straightened, and moved into a coffin.

"The way I figure it, all we need to do is get the coffin in the graveyard and we can start mining immediately! So, Crank! I know what we can do to speed up our fortune." He ripped his gloves off as though he could punctuate better with his hands.

"I got to figuring that there is poor McLeod laying in the meat house with all those critters, just waiting for Spring ... maybe even early-Summer for a decent burial. Right?"

Smooth's face had flushed with the thought of McLeod being cooped up with the a bunch of dismembered animals.

"So," said Smooth, "here's my plan. We're going to speed up the process. We get permission to plough a site in the graveyard and start melting the ground a little early. Remember when we melted-down through the ice to Jake McDonald's frozen water pipe?"

Crank looked confused. All he could remember was him accidentally clipping the corner of Jake's house with the edge of the D-8 Cat.

"Tyres!" Smooth exclaimed. "Don't you remember setting those tyres ablaze and adding to them until the ground thawed!"

"That took a lot of tyres. And we only had to thaw two feet down." Said Crank. "And six feet of frozen dirt is a long way!"

"Bad thinking!" Smooth scolded "It's simple, if you have a small idea that works, and a big problem, you just expand your little idea... more tyres!"

The town was growing impatient and their plans to winter in Florida, or maybe Cuba... anywhere but Lone Bull.

The Fenton boys' idea was generally approved by people they met on the street ranging from "Sure give her a try." to "Brilliant!" as bellowed by Simpson, the Town's town-scribe who collected stories from the pub side of the General Store, then added them in his cabin to "The Book!"

And so the Fenton brothers, with Council's consent, ploughed a route out to the Town Dump and specifically to the "used tyre" area.

To get there they had to plough a path into the discarded cars in which it was was generally understood that a grizzly had taken up hibernation there... though no one had seen it that year.

All went well as they navigated through the snowpack old cars, until suddenly out of a 1967 Ford Fairlane, its doors removed for access to the radio, Mr. Grizzly came stumbling out groggy but with an attitude! and it certainly didn't appreciate being awakened. Three big buckets full of old rimless rubbers tyres and a dead bear later, they got their first of many loads of rubber.

They started the thawing process, and then the rest of their time maintaining it. Six days tops the Fentons calculated. Not one thought was given to the fact that melt water was filling up the fire pit! Everyone turned out as the Fenton Brothers built a credible tower of tyres but with little thawed terrain results.

"You know" said Smooth realising that tyres need a lot of heat before they'll do anything. "There's an old Indian trick we can use, fill the tyres with diesel, so their walls will burn and make the fire burn hotter, and longer".

And it worked ... for a while giving the pyramid of tyres a Christmas tree look but as the fire melted the down the walls, the residual fuel flowed out onto the concrete-hard earth and travelled a long distance on the frozen surface.... quickly!

"HEY EVERYBODY!" cried Sally Miller, a young girl with a voice twice her age! Everyone turned and saw immediately that the excess fuel had puddled up against the meat storage building, and its corner was was now on fire!

They could cut off the fuel source, but they dared not touch the fire. Then Crank came up with an idea, "We'll have to cut a trench dissecting the fuel and drain it off the site."

Without further council, Smooth, who had only a vague notion of the plan, dropped the blade and started cutting a trench to divert the fuel.

But no sooner had he got started than someone hit his windshield with a snowball. Only on the second barrage of snowballs pelting them, did the brothers look around into the excited faces of a waving and yelling crowd of townsfolk, The Mayor leapt onto the cat-tracks and beat his fist on the engine cover screaming at them to stop and turn the machine off... which Smooth finally did.

"YOU IDIOTS!!" The Mayor yelled! "You have the blade at the wrong angle, ... you're channelling the fuel right into Lone Bull!"

The Mayor had to jump off the excavator's tracks as Smooth threw the gears into reverse. And, as the machine lunged backwards, he lifted the blade, opened the right cylinder compressor and the blade swung off-set 90 degrees... barely missing the fleeing Mayor..

Once a believer that the brothers were half-wits which collectively made a whole wit, the Mayor no longer supported that thesis.

The fuel now flowed directly towards town! Fortunately, the diesel never reached the Lone Bull divide but, instead it diverted down a ravine away from the Town! but still directly into the Lake.

"Ah! It's just 'collateral damage.' You got to expect something will occur, happens often in my business," was Fenton's rationale for not taking full responsibility for the problem.

There was one act of bravery in the calamity. Samson, the town 'lush' rushed into the burning meat house and grabbed the coffin and dragged it out.

When asked why he did such an act of bravery, he replied, "McLeod wanted a regular burial and not a cremation! I just want my money from the Will!"

Chapter 25

Cowboy Bob took them to Kennedy airport for their flight back to Lone Bull. He repeatedly thanked Maktu for taking the rap and saying that he was driving the car when the police caught them. If the police had charged him, he surely would have lost his driver's license.

New York to Vancouver, Vancouver to Whitehorse. The novelty had become tedious, and Maktu had become immune to travelling in tubes filled completely with strangers. Since their tickets were first class, and the plane to Vancouver was again a 747 with a lounge upstairs, they went there first, but even that seemed rather boring, having just, a few days before flown over New York City....at night, the towering skyscrapers ablaze with lights. Also, he was ready to go home. From Vancouver, they changed planes and immediately the terrain below was tall ice scoured mountain peaks with glaciers cross-hatched with deep crevasses.

Two hours out of Vancouver, with Haida Gwaii to the West, the plane suddenly turned due East towards the mainland and in a short time began descending slowly until they were once again flying over the rugged Coastal Range, and soon, on their trajectory there was a large lake with a few homestead farms along the western shoreline, the "Landers farms" he suspected.

The plane continued flying East above the lake when suddenly Christina grabbed Maktu's arm.

"Look! There's your cabin!"

Maktu looked across her and out of the window. "Our cabin. You're my partner now!" He placed his hand on her arm showing her his gold ring they had bought at Tiffany's. She grinned, "We will have to see a judge one of these days to actually marry us .... Someday!"

In Whitehorse they were met by a pilot who introduced himself and said that Chance had contacted him about flying them over the mountains to Lone Bull.

Picking up their bags he led them through the airport to the Western side where there was an 'Islander' eight passenger fixed-wing airplane. Beside it stood two young men in their late twenties who were also going to Lone Bull.

"Geologists." Maktu commented.

"How can you tell?" Asked Christina.

"By their backpacks. See the rock hammers and ice axes tied to the sides? But there is hope... see those two metal cylinders? Fly-rods for fishing!"

It was a beautiful day as they lifted out of Whitehorse. The plane circled for altitude above the mountains and then turned due West following the road over the pass to Lone Bull.

Days earlier two backhoes, Smooth's from the Lone Bull side of the mountain pass and one from Whitehorse, had opened the road and once again there was a scheduled transit bus that connected Whitehorse and Lone Bull. They were too anxious to get home to take it. Also, with the coming Spring and the annual influx of tourists and expat homeowners, there was now in fact this scheduled flight from Whitehorse to Lone Bull, though that day there were only four of them on it.

As the plane flew over the pass, Maktu saw that the summit

had been excavated and backhoe tracks across the alpine valley extended beyond the sides of the road, and there were signs that there had been a number of vehicle tracks spidering around it.

"FUCK!" He yelled so loudly that even the pilot heard him through his headphones.

Christina had been anticipating this moment since yesterday when she spoke to Mrs. Tashoots. Maktu was having such a wonderful experience she hadn't wanted to spoil it.

"I spoke with Mrs. Tashoots this morning." She was the woman looking after Shag. "She told me."

"And how is he?"

"Getting fat on a steady diet of caribou." She laughed, then fell silent, but suddenly she gave his arm a hard squeeze.

"They found Chris!" She blurted out. "When they were clearing the Pass, they found debris from his chopper. They figure it exploded when he crashed into the West wall of Tiki Peak. I learned about Chris's crash yesterday from Mrs. Tashoots, but since there was nothing, we could do from New York...and truthfully, I didn't want to cloud your success and our wonderful adventure, that's why I didn't tell you."

"No," he squeezed her hand. "Don't apologise, there was nothing we could have done from there!" Again, he fell silent.

"Fuck!" He swore again. "It must have happened when Chris was coming down the Lake to pick me up at the cabin when he crashed!"

Maktu knew who it was and likely what happened. As he looked closer at the ground he saw a bent helicopter main rotor blade. There was no mistaking it was Chris's by the stripes on the tip of the blade. Chris and he had painted them on the tips so Chris could judge how close or how far he was from the terrain in bad weather. Emergency rescue often was into tight places or bad weather. But that day down at Maktu's cabin it was neither bad weather, nor a crisis, in fact just the opposite.

Christina placed her hand on Maktu's arm. "They found the wreckage at the summit only a few days ago." She hesitated then spoke again.

"Wanda Tashoots said Smooth, the backhoe driver, had found pieces of helicopter debris when they were opening the road over the summit to Whitehorse that was closed by the avalanches the day Chris disappeared. She said Smooth saw a reflection of light and went to investigate and there was a tail section sticking up through the snow and rock face. It was a massive explosion that probably triggered the chain of avalanches that circled the Lake! They think the helicopter exploded on impact.... His body hasn't been found."

"Fuck!" Maktu screamed silently to himself.

Maktu suspected that Chris was an adrenaline junkie when he was alone. One-time Maktu noticed an audiotape in the machine's deck of Wagner operas!

"Kettle drums and Tempest" Chris had said.

Still, odd music for flying around in the sky like a winged bird. And when asked further about it, Chris' response was "A habit I picked up flying in Vietnam."

Chris had learned to fly in the U.S. Airforce and had been in Vietnam flying helicopters before coming to the Canadian Northwest.... "I was like a Loomis driver... Delivery and Recovery of troops." He'd told Maktu.

At first his missions entailed just moving supplies to "Outreach Squads". Then it got a lot more dangerous delivering and retrieving troops "behind enemy lines." "In Vietnam" Chris once told him, "Everywhere was behind enemy lines!"

"In fact, when I was flying in 'Nam', the first thing I'd do before going in on either a "delivery" or a "rescue" mission was focus on exactly where my gunner sat and on the first pass, we'd 'soften the jungle' with machine gun fire."

"It was on those occasions that I'd put in that tape in the deck.... Wagner sets the mood.... Mmmmm. Maybe I'm just an adrenaline junkie. After 'Nam' I feel at times like I'm bullet proof!"

"Maybe that's why I have a rule to never put the tape in when I'm going into, or, returning from a rescue mission with passengers."

"Even in Canada, if I am alone coming into a tight place, like a narrow valley where you can either climb above or take a line of sight and follow it... I put Wagner on!"

"Fuck!" Maktu swore again, but this time silently under his breath and only Christina felt his anger. He knew that Chris had died, taking unnecessary chances.

"I'm sorry." She whispered and gave his hand a gentle squeeze.

He pulled away, feeling first it was somehow his fault for being Chris's destination that fateful day. But he knew in his heart that his friend was a casualty of a forgotten War... hidden from history but forever written on the hearts of the survivors.

As they circled into the Valley and dropped down onto the airstrip at Lone Bull, Christina saw below that there was a large gathering at the Lone Bull graveyard.

"They must be burying McLeod." She said, looking out the window.

When they'd landed, Maktu went to the pick-up he'd shared with Chris. The keys were in it, and it started immediately.

"Want a ride?" He asked the two young men. His earlier observation was correct, they were geologists as he'd thought by the fact, that when they threw their packs into the truck, with its soft leaf-springs, it sagged significantly, the consequence of a geologist's gear. Also, going into town, sandwiched four across the front seat, they confirmed that they had been hired by "Mother

Load Mining," a gold exploration company out of Vancouver, to poke around McLeod's claim.

Nothing is secret in the North, despite the vast absence of man. The connective tissue is the public radiophone, and bored gossip between bush-pilots, who'd discussed McLeod willing his mine to the people of the Lone Bull Valley. The hook that caught the attention of Mother Load was that McLeod paid his bills in gold!

The town was empty. Everything was closed. They stopped at the grocery Store. "Tell Mable, if she's there that you'd like to rent a room, and she will find you a bed."

Christina and Maktu left their bags in the back of the pick-up. The thought that someone might steal something in Lone Bull was unthinkable.

Christina took his hand as they walked up the hill to the graveyard. "It's necessary." She said, as they started up.

The hard part of the revelation that Chris was dead and not on a rescue mission, came when Maktu realised that his friend was actually coming to Maktu's to sling out some of the painter's gear... in particular his paintings to Lone Bull and ultimately destined for New York.

Suddenly, the scenario of what had happened came upon Maktu. That time, in the early morning, the mountain pass would be full of fog.

"Once again we've thwarted Death!" Was Chris' expression when he had to go through tight places and there was no other choice. But Maktu knew there was something else... after Vietnam, Chris was an adrenaline junkie!

As they drew near the Town's graveyard, Maktu realised that the view from the graveyard was spectacular! He wondered why graveyards often have the most spectacular views. Even in cities they are parks often with landscaped gardens. He wondered if placing a graveyard wasn't founded on the principle that tranquillity is not for the dead, but the mourners left behind.

Drawing close to McLeod's grave, Maktu saw there were two gravestones.

James Arnold McLeod

Born: 1972 Died: March 2025

Gold Miner

The second stone read:

Chris Stapleton
Born: Oct 8, 1988
Died: March 18, 2025

Bush Pilot

Father Armiel, the Pentecostal Minister from Whitehorse was in charge of the services. "I didn't know McLeod well, in fact, the only time I'd laid eyes on him was when he took the Lone Bull bulldozer and tried to flatten the Town... including, if you can imagine, the Church!" He exclaimed.

The Priest shook his head... "including the church!" he repeated. "What had God ever done to him to warrant that!" He shook his head.

The priest then realized that he was "bad-mouthing" one of god's creatures and returned to the service. "He was a loner, and truthfully I can't say much more except that he was a philanthropist!"

"Now some people bequeath upon their death, money, land precious objects... but McLeod chose a hole that he, and he alone laboured in. In short, he was a dreamer... and shouldn't we all dream? I'd like to think that the way he lived out there alone...," the Priest elevated his voice. "That he was a dreamer... a pursuer of a dream." His eyes scanned the audience. "And I want to think that even when he found it, he kept on digging!" There was a long pause.

"May we pursue his dream wisely. Amen"

"Amen!" The gathering responded.

"Is there anyone else who would like to add something?" Asked the Mayor.

No one spoke.

Maktu squeezed Christina's hand. He'd never spoken in public, but this time he knew he had to and cleared his throat for attention. Christina held his hand tightly for support.

"Look! It's Maktu!" A child spoke up.

"I did not know Mcleod, though he was my neighbour... by twenty miles! But I did know Chris very well and I'd like to say a few words about him."

"We are all indebted to Chris for coming to rescue us when an emergency occurred."

There was a murmur of affirmation that ran through the gathering.

His voice faltered for a moment, but he knew he could not be timid this time! "And for that alone, all of us owe him our gratitude .... Even our lives!"

"I've lost a friend to whom I personally owe so much ... as we all do."

He fell silent but Christina squeezed his hand.

"Give thanks that Chris was in our lives." Maktu spoke again. His words were excruciating, but as his Grandmother used to say, "There are necessary things that must be done and words that must be said!"

"Well, my parting words of tribute are "Give Thanks" I, in particular for having had him in my life."

"He was my 'teacher'. When he'd drop by, he taught me about life in the outside world. And most of all, encouraged me to, as they say ... "pull the rope", ... take risks. For me, being raised in a very remote Indian village by my grandparents where English was a second language, if spoken at all, Chris gave me the tools to expand my horizons, my dreams. Take risks and go for your dreams even if they are in the 'outside world' and you have to go in it." He stood silently for a moment.

"Specifically for me, painting is my life, and it was Chris who not only encouraged me to do it, but show some of them to a gallery in Whitehorse, and, it was through that showing that they were seen by a gallery owner in New York."

"I guess the owner must have liked what he saw because he bought all that was there, and he offered me a show. And, as many of you know, I." he paused, turned and looked at Christina. "We just returned from the opening in New York.... And I guess it went very well... I've brought none home!"

"Ironically, even that was possible because Chris taught me so much about the outside world... even which dining-utensils to use for a fancy party." He laughed. "In fact, it was Chris who taught me how to read... though my spelling is not that good." He laughed again, looked at Christina with a smile, and held up his undamaged right hand showing his wedding ring. There was a murmur that ran through the gathering.

"So," he continued, "armed with the confidence I got from Chris, my bride and I just returned from the Big City and survived!"

"I have one last thought... a piece of advice, one piece of advice from Chris, that I always follow... 'Take risks, calculated but risks all the same'."

His emotions were getting too strong, Chance saw this. "Thank you, Chris, your memory and our gratitude will always be fresh... we are all indebted!" He had said what many felt, and there were many in tears.

Recognising that the service was over, the Priest closed with a prayer for departed souls.

Immediately many of the congregation gathered around Maktu thanking him for saying what they all felt.

“So?” asked Mayor Jarvis, “What was New York like?”

“About like here, but totally diffcrent!” He laughed.

Chance studied Maktu. There was something different, something had changed. It wasn’t the mountaineering glasses that Maktu now wore due to his accident at the lake... nor the ‘City’ haircut. He stood more erect.

No, something had changed! Adding to the shrinkage he generally adopted out of shyness, he didn’t make eye contact down pat. Maktu would fold forward slightly at the hips, though he was a tall man but not socially confident having been raised in an extremely remote and isolated part of the wilderness. Not accustomed to being the part of a conversation. Maktu seldom spoke, mainly because English was a second, if not third, language if you included the sounds of Nature. There was nothing wrong with Maktu’s hearing.

Maktu was a solidly built man. His character mirrored his life in the Wild, his features were strongly Native features. Somehow now he looked more socialised, more comfortable around people. After all, he had gone out ...to New York! And survived!

Chance had encouraged him that he could go to the City, return alive, and even enjoy it.

“Master Maktu”, one of the Permitter children came up to him.

“Why do you wear those funny glasses?” The boy asked.

“My eyes have been damaged. The sunlight is still painful, so the glasses are to stop the light.” It was enough of an answer for the boy.

"But it is still me." He lifted his glasses and the boy gasped! The skin around his eyes was still severely wrinkled, pitted, rooster red and puffy. The child gasped and drew back.

"You should see the other guy!" Maktu smiled and lowered his glasses.

The shock of being back after seeing New York running at full speed, and the success of the show, it all seemed a lifetime away against the hard reality that Chris was dead, and that Chris had died en route to pick him up was startling. And though the two friends experiences carried a strong measure of good memories, it was as if it were a dream.

"It was not your fault." Christina took his hand as they left the graveyard.

"Let's go," whispered Maktu to Christina, "and retrieve my dog."

"Your dog!" Christina growled. "He's our dog now! Our cabin. Our dog!"

"Cabins." Maktu corrected.

Someone saw the wedding rings and Maktu and Christina confirmed that they were now married, which sparked the same whispered responses, "I knew it would happen when they first met."

"I saw that was going to happen at the dance." Mrs Tashoots said to Bunny Fenton, Smooth's wife. "In fact, I'm privately elated." For she knew both before they knew each other.

"Christina married him for his dog."

"Shag's a great dog! I'm told he saved Maktu's life the night he crashed!"

"You notice the dog is getting a little fat at the Tashoots house."

"It could be the dog food diet he was on when Maktu was in the hospital."

"So, what will you remember most about New York?" Asked Brand as they left the graveyard.

"Noise!" Maktu said with certainty. "That and everything there is manufactured! The buildings are manufactured out of concrete and held together with manufactured steel. Most transportation is on manufactured rails, cars and buses".

He thought for a moment. "Even the air in most of the skyscrapers is pre-conditioned before you breathe it. But it is the noise that is the most pervasive. In fact, you can hear street-noise all the way to the top of the Empire State Building, and that is a quarter of a mile high in the air from the street!

"Listen Up!" He said . All did.

"I don't hear anything!" A little boy blurted out.

"Exactly!" Maktu smiled. "Here you can think in silence. In New York it is a continual background noise even late at night! Continual sirens some-place. Ambulances on emergency calls, police chases."

He looked at Christina and gave a quick smile. With much to think about, the gathering began to disperse, Mayor Jarvis spoke up.

"Attention everyone!" He called before the mourners departed for Lone Bull and K'weset.

"As you likely know, in terms of McLeod's Will, following a proper burial of his body, which we just had, he willed us his gold mine. But now, the question is: How do we equally share a mine?" No one had thought about it. "That's when we came up with the idea of shares to which we've printed enough that everyone get an equal amount, all adult-age folks of both Lone Bull and K'weset, and the down-lake 'Landers'. And then to regulate the transaction of them, we are going to set up our own 'stock exchange' where the price is set by demand for them at the moment."

He looked around the audience to see if they were aware of the concept of Shares and a stock exchange. "To this end we are calling the company 'The Lone Bull Bonanza'".

"Mrs. Brand has designed and printed Share certificates which you should all be able to pick up at the Town Offices in a week.

"I don't understand." There was a little confirming discussion before the Mayor spoke again. "So, the way this works is that a share has an initial value, and as a benchmark for the purpose of selling them in the future we have set a price of $1.00."

"Now, to facilitate share transactions I will make up a black board which will sit in the General Store's front window with the most recent share price. And to start the initial transactions, each share will have its own certified number. Each transaction will be registered by my wife Mabel, who will act as a Controller and keep a record of each transaction, and I'll post on the blackboard in the Store's window the latest selling price. Questions?"

"What if I sell my shares for more.... or maybe less than the posted price?"

"That's up to you. The reason we are suggesting posting the transactions on the board, is to set up an idea of current exchange rates as a guidance for future transactions. I call it the 'The Bull Stock market!'"

"I think the 'Bullshit Stock Exchange' would be more appropriate!" Shouted Smooth Fenton from the group.

"Yah" said Jason Peters, a retired miner who had remained in Lone Bull with his wife, living on their retirement fund. "I'll buy all your shares for a buck a share!"

"Sold!" Said Bently Johnson.

"Great!" Said Chance. "BUT! I will have to run all this past the Yukon Attorney general... but when it is legally structured, we will now have an opening price of a dollar a share and I will post the transaction on 'The Board'. I'll put it in the store window. However, judging by the phone and fax messages, there is a lot of excitement over McLeod's mine from the outside! So, DO NOT SELL TOO SOON!"

As the gathering walked down the hill to Lone Bull and beyond to K'weset, the idea of stocks and a Stock Exchange, and that the terms of McLeod's will had been met, and now that each person had shares, the Mine's future became the topic of conversation down from the graveyard.

"You know what I am going to do with my proceeds from the Will?" Said Mrs. Walker, a long-time resident whose husband had died of Black Lung Disease back when the mine was still operating.

"I'm going to move to Florida and buy a condominium in one of those retirement homes and have my grandchildren come to visit. No one ever comes to see me in Lone Bull."

"Not me!" Interjected Mrs. Casper, also a widow to Black Lung Disease said to her best friend of Mrs. Walker, "I'm taking my Grands to Disneyland!" She grinned.

"Well," said Mrs. Thompson, whose husband had also died of Black Lung! "I'm going to a fantasy restaurant where a penguin-dressed waiter actually comes to your table and takes your order for food cooked to your preference. Frankly, I'm tired of either wild game meat, or canned meat like 'Spam' and particularly boiled, shrivelled-up vegetables. I can't tell you how long it has been since I tasted an orange or even a fresh apple."

"Would you be interested in teaching a painting class?" A lady from the Lone Bull Auxiliary asked Maktu. He was silent thinking about such a novel idea.

"I can't!" He said finally. "I've never had lessons myself!"

"In fact, all I could say is what my Grandmother taught me.

Paint what you feel and not just what you see." Then he laughed. "In New York, there are artists that paint only what they feel!"

He thought about his words. "See that pinecone? I could paint it exactly, but that would not show what I feel. I'm more interested in focusing on that raindrop on the pinecone." He stopped, searching for the right words. "I'm more interested when the picture of the pine-cone is filtered through the light as it is broken down into rainbows and giving me a feeling of the whole; the pine-cone, the water droplet and the rainbows."

He stopped abruptly. He loved applying what his Grand taught but a class? "No, I would not be able to instruct." He smiled. "For a number of reasons. First my wife and I will no longer be living here, we're going down to my cabin."

Suddenly Christina became delighted with the idea. She too thought he should teach, if for no other reason than his Grandmother's teaching. It had certainly worked for Maktu.

"Why not a workshop, say in the summer at our place," Christina interjected into the conversation.

"Bring a tent and a contribution to a common food stash. Anyway, that would be fine with me, if it works for Maktu." She smiled. Maktu agreed, but he didn't know if he could teach anything except what he learned from his Grandma Shula.

That settled, Christina gave Maktu a squeeze. "Let's go and retrieve my dog."

"Your dog?" Maktu growled. "He's our dog now! Our cabin, Our dog!"

"I'll have to find a replacement nurse, but that shouldn't be difficult, I'm told there's a line-up."

Dropping off their suitcases at Christina's cabin, they hurried over to K'weset Village to pick up Shag. And though he was excited to see them, he was clearly reluctant to leave, and he came with them on a leash having had a steady diet of wild game, even fresh dead meat rotting from last fall's run. Now that the Lake ice had sunk, there were large sections of more dead fish. And what the village dogs miss, the bear and maggots got fat on.

Chapter 26

By late summer there really was nothing substantial to show at the Lone Bull Mine. The young geologists had to tunnel through the avalanche's debris into the main shaft of McLeod's mine. And though it took over a week of hard digging and shovelling snow and mud, plus boulders the size of refrigerators out of the conglomerate ... and then studying the walls of the shaft very closely, they found no trace of a gold seam, the mine was barren!

But... the fishing was great!

Their telegram came through the Company's satellite phone. It read, "*Promising, VERY promising!* Will report back soon! Need fresh supplies! Use the Company card?"

Already the 'Company', had leased a boat and motor that was listed as "essential transportation" even though it was exclusively for going fishing in a different inlet each day.

In fact, when the boys discovered the perfect 'hand-tied' fishing flies, they soon found that they could catch more than they could eat, and they started trading fish to Earnie Big Bear in exchange for smoked caribou and salmon. Similarly, they traded fish for vegetables with Mrs. Muller who had a garden that was so abundant, it fed her family of six with plenty left over.

"And we're getting paid for this?" The young men marvelled.

However, they did still carry their stone hammers on their fishing ventures just in case another crew of geologists appeared, and the boys had to look busy. There was no concern coming from the local fishermen about their full-time pastime, the Lake was bountiful.

"Michael, It is Marvin." The stockbroker Marvin Evans spoke in a calm business-as-usual voice into the phone receiver just as though he and Michael were still having their conversation over lunch at the Vancouver Club.

"Good to hear you too." He said.

"So, I have something that might interest you. You did very well with my last tip didn't you?" He waited for a reply.

"Great! So here is the deal." Evans said.

"The two young geologists we sent up have explored the shit out of this Lone Bull miner's claims and once the people of that Valley form a company and meet the terms of his Will, we'll quietly buy up controlling shares. The way I see it, it's a gamble but the miner McLeod may have hit gold! And as I see it we can slowly get control of the Lone Bull Company by buying the locals' shares. Then once the Company is certified, we float the rumour around the Vancouver Club that the mine is really a bonanza! Then we quietly sell our shares at a profit and make a lot of money without having to lift a pick and shovel!"

"Great!" He responded to Michael's encouraging response. Evans sat back at his office desk thinking about McLeod's mine and the company shares idea that the locals had set up. It was certainly a point of interest.

He listened to Michael's excited response. "Wonderful! You're in!"

Then, just as he'd finished the phone conversation, Robert, one of his staff from the 'Research' Department' burst into the office.

"Boss, I found something that might interest you about that Lone Bull property. It's newspaper clipping from the "Whitehorse Star, March,1928."

"Basically, it reports that a "giant" earthquake in the mountains West of Whitehorse occurred around the Lone Bull Mountain, essentially closing the already abandoned Lone Bull mine!"

"The report went on to say geologists believe that a large section of the Lone Bull Mountain physically "dropped" as much as a hundred meters!" He stopped reading the report from the paper.

"Isn't that roughly the level where that miner from Lone Bull was tunnelling on the 'back' side of the mountain?"

"I'll be damned!" Evans barked and sat upright. "Maybe, just 'maybe' that old sourdough was right in thinking the gold seam that the Lone Bull Company was working, just dropped and the gold seam carried through on the other side!"

He thought for a moment. "Maybe we should intensify our field work there!"

That information, plus the recent news he'd heard from a subsidiary out of Whitehorse confirming that the miner had in fact willed his claim including title, to the people in the Lone Bull and K'weset Village, and that they had formed a company and were issuing shares to everyone who lived there was very interesting.

And, even if the mine was a dud, they still got the rights to it cheap, and in a bullish market he and Michael could flog it further around the 'Club'.

He called Michael back with his thoughts on the venture and listened to Michael's response.

"Exactly! That's when we release the 'Promising, Very Promising!' geologists report... and maybe add a few superlatives of our own".

"Right now, the Valley folks haven't opened the listing anywhere. But the shares will be peanuts when they are listed on the Vancouver Exchange!"

He listened to the response.

"My thoughts exactly! And after the issuances, we can get control without having put out very much capital. And if the mine is profitable, by getting controlling shares, we can control the whole operation."

Evans listened to Michael's encouraging response and then remembered. "Oh! Something else, I just got a message from our geologist team up North, three short words.... 'Promising, VERY promising!' And the "Very" is underlined"

"So, here is the deal. We'll keep the geologist there into fall, offer them a time and a half wage increase that they can't refuse. Say whatever it takes to keep them exploring. And at the same time, we quietly start buying up control of the issued shares from the people of the Valley!"

He stopped for a long silence as he listened to Michael's reaction.

"Exactly! I agree, rumour is a good way to make money in this business."

"So, see you for lunch at the Club on Wednesday?" He hung up, pleased. His friend Michael would be in for two million, if for nothing else then they could control the future of the mine, even if it was barren. In his business, control of the rights to a piece of land is a form of ownership without having to turn a shovel! Consequently, rumours can make a venture profitable, even if there's no substance to them!

Back at Lone Bull, when the two geologists got the message to extend their efforts for a wage increase, they decided to focus exclusively on fly-fishing full time. Geologically they'd found nothing .... nor around, the mine, was there even any quartz deposits which often trap fine-gold inside their crystal lattice.

"Still Promising!" Read their next email. "Unfortunately, we have to calculate extra expenses and an additional thirty percent would be necessary for fall supplies. Still very promising, and we still hope to find one vein that maybe the main artery!"

When Evans got their reply, he was driving home. His road to wealth was not illegal, and really only slightly unethical. But in his business, ethics is a slippery slope... all the way to the bank! It was what he called, "Marketing the Imagination" with information an investor wants to hear!

Chapter 27

As Christina sat with Shag on the boat-dock at K'weset harbour watching the homemade freighter-boat coming into the Bay, as it ran on both a small outboard motor and large black and white with checker board sails, she marvelled at how much her life had changed since she stood there on the beach watching the K'weset Village men with a backhoe and chains, pulling Maktu's snowmobile out of the ice crushed shoreline. She thought about the dog sitting beside her and how he had dragged the man to her cabin's doorstep, and how that single act had changed her life forever... at least, she hoped forever... no, she thought further that's not right, it will be forever... the consequence of destiny, and also because she had news!

She remembered that lone, brutally cold night writing to her best friend Kay how boring life was in the "Great Canadian North", and how she may have made a terrible mistake and marvelled how much her life had changed in less than a year, nine months, to be exact. Changed from sitting around a swimming pool in her family's home in Bryn Mawr, Pennsylvania with her pet cocker-spaniel, to waiting on a dock in northern Canada with a huge dog of many generations of mongrels, which she suspected had at least one wolf in the mix,

She smiled thinking about how much her life had changed from the sheltered manicured estates of Bryn Mawr, Pennsylvania to the calamity on her doorstep that night... the howling dog, the man barely alive. Never before in her sheltered upbringing could she have anticipated that moment AND be so exquisitely fulfilled to be there in it!

Three of her girlfriends from childhood came to Maktu's showing at the Sullivan Gallery. All lived within a few blocks of each other in nearby Pennsylvania, but as well, close to where they were born and raised. All of them had counselled seriously and strenuously not to take a teaching position in a remote region of the planet on the West Coast, isolated even by Canadian standards.

Still, each of them confided confidentiality that they were bored, and asked if Christina wasn't deathly bored so far from "civilisation".

She laughed. "Civilisation is a value judgement usually made by someone looking for more of it." Christina laughed. "Sure, I don't have a television, nor do any of my neighbours. But, how often has any one in Bryn Mawr ladies had a community dance that ended with breakfast?" The weight of her argument rose dramatically when at the Sullivan Show they met Maktu. No, and, confident within his skin, he was only more handsome, shy, and devoted to Christina, than they had in their own lives.

"Moreover!" She said to Shag, "He has us to look after him." She giggled to the dog, for she could think of no other man she ever knew from her Bryn Mawr past who could live so confidently in a land where humans are not the measure and usually but a mere oddity.

The freighter-boat rode much higher in the water coming home than it had going out loaded to the gunnels with the weight of a 'lift' of construction lumber, fourteen rolls of roofing, a generator and all the tools, necessary to build a new 'addition' onto Maktu's cabin – ultimately three times bigger than the original log cabin!

Also, there would be running, fresh water inside, and an indoor toilet. The outhouse would be kept if for no other reason than starwatching. She smiled to herself at the irony that it was a fortuitous extension, especially when Maktu heard the news that Christina had.

Both Christina and Shag leapt to their feet, excited when Maktu and his cousin "Reimown" landed at the boat dock. It had been almost four weeks since she last saw him headed off for "his" cabin.

"His"? No, that wasn' t right, "their" new house or at least one dramatically renovated. Christina was satisfied with the former cabin.

It seemed much longer than four weeks since he and his cousin went down to the cabin to expand it. Expand it significantly, adding three rooms, a separate kitchen... and at Christina's insistence, indoor plumbing.

Shag was so excited to see Maktu he leapt into the boat even before they tied off.

Maktu was surprised how much he had missed her. It was a new experience, except for his 'Grans', especially his Grandmother, no one gave any thought to him in their lives. No ... Chris did. Chris, she suspected, had made his friend a project. Made him comfortable in a social situation. He taught him how to read, how to write, and most of all paint with confidence. She marvelled at just how much confidence Maktu had in the City, even at his show.

He glanced over at the beach adjacent to the dock. He still marvelled that he had survived the crash, and that his dog had acted so courageously. For a moment, he looked at the woman waiting for him. The success of the show that had garnished him with enough money to expand his life and courage to include her! "Give thanks! Chris would counsel him. Give thanks!

As he looked at the woman on the dock as they came in,

he understood the feelings his Grandparents had for each other. In fact, when his Grandmother died from lingering diabetes, his Grandfather died a week later from a broken heart.

"I missed you so much!" Maktu surprised himself to express so much emotion in public. Except for the time Maktu was in the hospital in Whitehorse, Maktu and Christina had not been separated from each other since Shag dragged him to her door.

As they walked up the dock, holding hands, Christina suddenly stopped. "Shag and I have something to tell you." Christina said.

"As do I!"

"You first." He said.

"No, you first." She smiled.

"Well," Maktu said with a big grin on his face, his eyes sparkled. "We realised we had far too much lumber so..." He smiled at her, "so we decided to add another room! In fact, a second floor to the house... another bedroom! And..." He took her hand. "So now from our new upstairs master bedroom, we can see all of the surrounding mountain peaks, and all the way down the Lake to the Landers' farms and beyond to the Coast without having to get out of bed!"

He smiled at her excitement. "And you? What surprise do you and Shag have for me? Puppies?" He asked.

"Worse! And much more work!" She smiled.

"Babies!" She gave his hand a hard squeeze and watched as Maktu's face passed through confusion to bewilderedness to unrestrained joy. But then it froze with confusion.

"Plural?" He asked.

"The doctor says he thinks there are two of them! Twins!'"

Made in the USA
Coppell, TX
23 January 2026

69162725R00108